LL

THE BIG
Open

Center Point
Large Print

Also by Stan Lynde and available from Center Point Large Print:

Vendetta Canyon
To Kill a Copper King

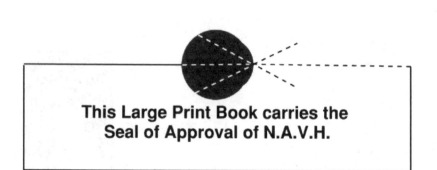

This Large Print Book carries the Seal of Approval of N.A.V.H.

THE BIG

A MERLIN FANSHAW WESTERN

STAN LYNDE

CENTER POINT LARGE PRINT
THORNDIKE, MAINE

This Center Point Large Print edition
is published in the year 2012 by arrangement with
Kleinworks Agency.

The text of this Large Print edition is unabridged.
In other aspects, this book may vary
from the original edition.
Printed in the United States of America
on permanent paper.
Set in 16-point Times New Roman type.

ISBN: 978-1-61173-532-1

Library of Congress Cataloging-in-Publication Data

Lynde, Stan, 1931–
  The big open : a Merlin Fanshaw Western mystery / Stan Lynde. —
Center Point large print ed.
   p. cm.
  ISBN 978-1-61173-532-1 (lib. bdg. : alk. paper)
  1. Fanshaw, Merlin (Fictitious character)—Fiction.
   2. United States marshals—Fiction. 3. Cowboys—Montana—Fiction.
    4. Ranchers—Montana—Fiction.
    5. Copper mines and mining—Fiction. 6. Large type books. I. Title.
PS3562.Y439B54 2012
813'.54—dc23
                                                          2012024573

To Lynda
Then and Now
The Wind beneath My Wings

THE BIG

One

A BULLET, ONCE FIRED

I never meant to kill the boy, but a bullet once fired doesn't care whose life it takes. On a dark April night in 1889, a slug from my forty-four took young Toby Slocum's life and changed my own forever.

I had come to Miles City at the behest of my boss, U.S. Marshal Chance Ridgeway. As his chief deputy, I served at the marshal's pleasure, and his pleasure seemed mostly to involve my going where he told me to go and doing what he told me to do. The marshal would arrive by train from Helena on the morning of April 3 and I was to meet him at the station. It's a well-known fact that only a fool or a newcomer predicts the weather in Montana, but I do believe April on the high plains may be the most treacherous month of all. So with that in mind, I saddled my Rutherford horse, threw my bedroll and a camp outfit on my roan, and set out for Miles City a day ahead of time.

A booster friend of mine used to say that while other places endure weather Montana enjoys climate. What's more, he said it with a straight face. Now I can't say I fully agree with his statement, but I have to admire his attitude. Optimism may not always lead to a successful outcome, but it does make the pursuit livelier. As luck would have it, the weather held good. I camped that night on Timber Creek, just west of the Mountain Sheep Bluffs, and rode into town the next afternoon.

Miles City was all a-bustle at the time. The annual meeting of the Montana Stockgrowers was in session, and local cattlemen and cowhands were thicker than fleas on a reservation dog. Representatives from the cattle-hauling Northern Pacific Railroad and the stockyards at St. Paul were on hand, as were cowmen from as far away as Texas and Canada. They were all gathered in Miles City to whoop and holler and let their wolf loose, but also to plan the spring cattle roundup across an area that covered a full third of Montana Territory.

Boasting well over fifteen hundred settlers, Miles City's four dozen saloons dispensed a thousand bottles of beer and four hundred gallons of whiskey every day, and catered to the high and low appetites of its citizens and visitors by way of a half-dozen brothels, opera houses, and other entertainments.

Freight wagons, buckboards, and carriages crowded the busy streets, as well as cowhands on horseback, soldiers from nearby Fort Keogh, and townspeople doing their marketing. Music drifted out from saloons and dance halls as I picked my way up the street past hitch racks crowded by tethered horses.

After putting my ponies up at Ringer and Johnson's Livery, I treated myself to a shave and haircut at a barber shop on Main Street. Then I walked over to the jail and paid a call on Tom Irvine, long-time sheriff of Custer County. I found Tom at his desk and up to his elbows in paperwork. He greeted me with a broad grin and a handshake.

"It's good to see you again, Merlin," he said. "What brings you to the metropolis of eastern Montana?"

"My buckskin horse and a meeting with Chance Ridgeway," I said. "The old man's comin' in on the train tomorrow."

"Be good to see him," Tom said. "It's good to see *anyone* who can take me away from this paperwork for awhile."

Tom came out from behind his desk. "I expect you could eat a bite. What say we have a few beers over at Charlie Brown's and a plate of his mulligan stew?"

I smiled. "Eatin' is my favorite sport," I said. Tom Irvine was a seasoned-looking man, heavy of build, with the long mustaches most men wore in those days. He had quick, piercing eyes, and the wind-burned look of a man who spent much of his time out-of-doors. Tom had the reputation of being a dogged and honest lawman, keeping the peace in a vast and mostly empty region. In those days, Custer County extended all the way from the Dakotas to Bozeman, Montana, a greater area than some eastern states.

Charlie Brown's Saloon was a single story log building at the corner of Fifth and Main, just across the street from Jimmy Coleman's Cottage Saloon, where most of the soldiers from Fort Keogh spent their pay. Charlie Brown was quite the character. Big-hearted and open-handed, he served as veterinarian, justice of the peace, and auctioneer for the town. He also ran a livery stable and traded horses in addition to managing the saloon that bore his name. In the saloon's back room, Charlie kept a tin boiler of mulligan stew simmering on the stove night and day, free to anyone who was hungry.

He was behind the bar when Tom and me walked in. "Who da hell sent for da peace officers?" Charlie asked. "Dis place got enough dam deadbeats already!"

Tom grinned. "We came in here against our better judgment," he said, "to abuse our stomachs. Bring us a couple bowls of your mulligan and two cold beers. Lucky for you I'm in a good mood. I might even pay you this time."

Charlie's grin matched Tom's. "Oh hell, I suppose I better. You'll probably *arrest* me if I don't—send me off to da prison at Deer Lodge."

Charlie turned to me. "You look like a decent feller," he said. "What da hell you hangin' around *dis* bum for? He's crooked, you know—crooked as a gully!"

I dealt myself in on their good-natured game. "Oh, I know he is," I said. "I'm takin' crooked lessons from him so *I* can run for sheriff."

Tom pulled out a chair at a deal table and sat down. "Meet Merlin Fanshaw, Charlie," he said. "Merlin is chief deputy to Chance Ridgeway."

Charlie's handshake was firm. "Ach, Ja. I know Marshal Ridgeway," he said. "*Gut* man. Welcome to Charlie Brown's."

With that, Charlie stepped behind the bar, drew two beers, and set them before us. Then he disappeared into the back room and returned with two steaming bowls of stew, a plate of hot sourdough biscuits, and a bowl of butter. "Eat hearty, boys," he said, and went back to his place behind the bar.

Tom picked up a biscuit, tossing it from hand to hand until it cooled enough to eat. "Well," he said. "You heard the man. Eat hearty."

I picked up a biscuit myself. "I can do that," I said.

We finished our meals. We ordered a second round of beers and then a third. We lingered long, getting acquainted as men will. I had met Tom on a previous trip to Miles City but we'd

13

never talked at length. I found him to be a gifted storyteller and his tales of hunting buffalo during the last years of the great northern herds, of horses he'd used and owned, and of outlaws he'd pursued, kept us late at the table as night fell and the streets grew dark.

Customers came and went. Charlie Brown made his way through the saloon, lighting the big coal-oil lamps that hung above the tables. A few sports bucked the tiger at a faro layout across the room. Near the front doors, a draw poker game plodded on. Two dancehall girls, well past their maidenhood, drank together at a table, their faces haggard and sad in the lamplight.

"Well," Tom said. "I expect we ought to call it a day. You've had a long ride and I reckon you could use some shut-eye. I can fix you up with a bed down at the jail if you like."

"I'd appreciate that," I said. "I'll need to be bright-eyed and bushy-tailed when I meet Ridgeway in the mornin'."

Leaving Charlie Brown's was a step from lamplight into darkness. Away from the Main Street saloons, Miles City slept under overcast skies with neither moon nor stars to light the gloom. Here and there, street lamps cast pale circles of light, but there seemed neither rhyme nor reason to their locations or their numbers.

With Tom leading the way, we walked along the empty street. A cold breeze met us as we went, and I shivered in spite of myself. Gradually, my eyes adjusted to the dark and I found the going easier. Then Tom stopped suddenly and I nearly ran into him. He stood tall, his attention fixed on a two-story brick building a block away. "Funny," he said. "I thought I saw a light over yonder. That's the State National Bank. Shouldn't be anyone there this time of night."

"Want to have a look?" I asked.

Tom nodded. "That's what they pay us for."

The State National Bank occupied a city lot at the corner of Eighth and Pleasant Streets. A single smoky street lamp guttered at its west side, casting a glow upon the building. We approached the bank by way of the alley, walking cat-footed and careful. Ten yards farther on, Tom stopped again. Pointing, he whispered, "There! The shade's drawn, but there's a light on inside, sure enough!"

I looked where Tom was pointing. A thin strip of lamplight shone in the window between the sill and the lower edge of the shade.

In the shadows behind the bank, something moved. I held my breath. As I watched, a horse and rider eased into the flickering light of the street lamp. The rider drew rein with his right hand, halting the paint horse he rode, and I saw that he held the reins of two other saddled horses in his left hand. He appeared to be a big man, his features hidden by a broad-brimmed hat and the turned up collar of his canvas duster.

I took hold of Tom's sleeve. "Look there, behind the bank," I whispered. "There's a man on horseback, and he's holdin' two *other* horses!"

"I see him," Tom said. "What do you think, Deputy?"

"I think banker's hours have either been moved up to midnight or there's a robbery in progress."

Tom nodded. "That's what I think, too. Keep an eye on that bird while I go *frustrate* this felony."

"All right," I said. "Watch yourself."

Crouching low, Tom disappeared around the corner into the darkness. I turned my attention back to the man in the duster. Still clutching the bridle reins of the riderless horses, he lounged carelessly in the saddle.

I held my breath. The man seemed unaware of my presence but his horse caught my scent. Tossing its head, the animal danced a nervous quickstep.

I heard the throbbing of my heart. My mouth was dry as I drew my forty-four from its leather. I stood up and stepped into the light.

"U.S. Marshal," I said. "Hold it right there!"

My sudden appearance didn't seem to startle the man. Slowly, he turned his head toward me. And *smiled.*

"Hands up!" I said. But his smile only widened. He thrust his free hand inside his duster.

"Don't *do* it," I warned. "*Raise* 'em!"

His hand swept out, pointed toward me. By the

glow of the street lamp I caught the glint of metal! *Gun,* I thought.

The forty-four bucked in my hand. Flame belched from its muzzle, the sound of the shot loud in my ears. My bullet struck the man high in the chest and threw him backward. Frightened, his horse bolted, its rider slipping from the saddle. The reins of the led horses burned through his fingers and he fell heavily onto the rutted street.

I was on him in an instant. His hat fell off and I was surprised to see he was merely a boy, and not a man at all! He lay on his back, eyes wide and staring into mine. He clutched his chest, where bright blood pulsed through his fingers and stained his duster. His face wore a surprised expression. *Why,* he seemed to ask, *why did you shoot me?*

I scanned the street for the weapon he'd drawn. And then I saw it, four feet away in the circle of light made by the street lamp. Bending, I picked it up. I could scarcely believe my eyes. The "weapon" was not a gun, after all, or even a knife. What I thought was a weapon was only a harmless thing of tin and wood—a battered *harmonica!*

I knelt beside the boy and saw at a glance he was hard hit. His bulging eyes asked questions I couldn't answer and panic rode him with its spurs on. His breathing came in ragged gasps and I heard the wheezing sound that bespoke a punctured lung. I bent over him, lifting his head up and out of the dirt. *"Easy,* kid," I said. "Rest easy."

"Easy" was the last thing on the boy's mind. Grasping my arm, he strained to pull himself up. A spasm seized him and his body stiffened. Then his breath left him in a long and ragged sigh and he fell back dead.

For a moment, I just knelt there in the dirt and stared. The kid had been maybe thirteen, no more than fourteen years old. He would never be older. The skin of his face was smooth and hairless as a girl's. He would never shave or grow a beard. His open eyes stared sightless at the sky above us. My hand trembled as I reached out and closed them. In the light of the street lamp the boy's blood looked black as oil. It had stained his duster and homespun shirt and had pooled in the dirt beneath him.

Swiftly, I searched his body. I found two glass marbles and a piece of chalk in his pocket, nothing else. Beyond those childish treasures the boy had carried only the well-worn harmonica. He carried neither pistol nor knife. He had not been armed with a weapon of any kind. A kind of baffled anger took me. *What kind of fool outlaw goes to a bank robbery unarmed?*

I got to my feet. The sound of men walking came from the darkness in front of the bank and I looked up to see two hard-looking hombres shuffling toward me with their hands up. Tom Irvine followed behind them, carrying a pair of belted revolvers and herding the men along at gunpoint. An older man with flyaway white hair and rimless spectacles walked beside Tom, wearing a bathrobe and carpet slippers.

"These two-bit thieves are Pete and Jack Slocum," Tom said. "They're crooked as snake tracks and dumb as gravel. Mostly, they steal their neighbors' chickens, pigs, and sometimes an occasional horse. I guess they figured they were ready for the big time."

Tom nodded at the white-haired gent. "Lucius here is the bank's head cashier. These boys abducted him from his hearth and home and forced him to come down here and open the vault."

Tom's eyes went to the body of the boy and then met mine again. "I heard a shot," he said. "Are you all right?"

I looked down at the boy's still form. "I'm all right," I said, "but the kid here isn't. I threw down on him and told him to raise his hands. Instead, he reached inside his duster and pulled out . . . what I thought was a gun."

My throat grew tight. For a moment I couldn't speak. Then I said, "I shot him out of the saddle, and he died where he fell. I never meant to kill him, Tom—but I reckoned it was him or me."

One of the two outlaws—I think it was Pete Slocum—suddenly saw the boy's body. "Gawd-amighty!" he bawled. "You done kilt Toby! You gunned down our baby brother!"

Tom looked closer. "That's *Toby?* You dumb bastards brought *Toby* along to help you rob a bank?"

Pete Slocum withered under Tom's scolding. "Hell, Tom," he said, "all we done was let him hold the horses!"

The other brother, Jack, chimed in. "That's right!" he said. "It was that *law dog* yonder kilt Toby—shot him down in cold blood!"

"Shut the hell up," Tom said. "You made Toby an accessory to kidnapping and armed robbery when you dreamed up this hare-brained stunt! Way I see it; *you* boys killed Toby!"

Jack Slocum shook his head. "That's too thin, Sheriff," he said. "Toby never had no pistol—that peace officer gunned down a harmless child!"

Tom prodded Jack in the belly with his gun barrel. "You know where the jail is," Tom said. "Move out!"

The Slocums turned away in the direction of the courthouse, with Tom and me behind them. Just as we turned to go, Tom glanced at me. He seemed to be taking my measure. Did I see *support* in his glance, or *doubt?*

The night policeman met us at the courthouse. "Lock these boys in a cell," Tom said. "Then wake up the coroner and send him to the State National Bank. Toby Slocum is there, dead in the street. And there are three saddle horses around there somewhere. See if you can round 'em up and take 'em over to Ringer and Johnson's."

Back in Tom's office, he poured me a cup of coffee and told me to pull up a chair. "Now," he said, "Tell me again how the shootin' went down."

"When you went inside the bank, I threw down on the kid . . . on Toby. I said I was a U.S. marshal and told him to raise his hands. Instead, he reached inside his duster and pulled out what I thought was a gun. He pointed it at me and I shot him. He died in less than a minute."

Tom nodded. "You say he pulled what you *thought* was a gun. If it wasn't a gun, what was it?"

I laid the harmonica on Tom's desk. "This," I said.

Tom nodded, his face grim. "Toby's harmonica," he said. "I'll be damned."

"No," I said. "*I* will. I killed an unarmed kid."

Tom frowned. "Let me tell you about the Slocum brothers," he said, "and about Toby's mouth harp. Pete and Jack run a hardscrabble horse ranch west of here on Scottie Creek. They run a few pairs of Texas cattle and trade horses with the unwary. They've been in my jail a time or two for rustlin' and horse theft but I've had to let 'em go for lack of evidence.

"When Toby was ten, he got kicked in the head by a fractious mule and came out of it with a sweet spirit and a simple mind. Pete and Jack used to bring Toby to town with 'em when they came in to drink whiskey and hump whores. Of course they didn't take him inside the saloon nor into the cat house neither.

"They used to set Toby out in front of the Keg Saloon while they drank and socialized. Toby never seemed to mind much; he just smiled and said howdy to the folks who passed by and waited for Pete and Jack to come out."

Tom picked up the harmonica from his desk. "Well, one day L.A. Huffman, the photographer, came by and gave Toby this harmonica. You'd have thought he'd gave him the moon! Toby sat outside, playin' tunes only he understood and showin' his harp off to everyone who walked by. Most everybody in town came to know about Toby and his harmonica."

Tom took a sip of his coffee. "When you braced him at the bank tonight, Toby didn't know he was part of a bank holdup. He figured you were just another stranger he could show his mouth harp to."

"Dear God," I said. "And I killed him for it."

"There's no way you could have known," Tom said. "What I said at the bank is true—Pete and Jack killed Toby when they brought him along on the bank job."

"That's cold comfort," I said. "Maybe if I hadn't been so quick to shoot . . ."

There was anger in Tom's voice. "Suppose the horse holder at the bank tonight had *not* been Toby but a bona fide man killer. If you *hadn't* been quick, you'd be dead now—and this conversation would not be takin' place."

"I expect you'll call a coroner's jury. I'll abide by what they decide."

"That's noble of you, but there'll be no jury. Toby Slocum met death by misadventure during an attempted holdup. That's all she wrote."

"But durn it, Tom, I . . ."

"Let me tell you a true story, Merlin. Back in the summer of '83, when this town was even wilder than it is now, a lowlife named Bill Rigney and one of his drinkin' pardners went on an all-night carouse and wound up in the better part of town. They broke into the home of a man named Campbell while he was at breakfast with his wife and daughter. Campbell ordered the trespassers to leave and they refused. Rigney and his cohort then began to abuse the ladies with foul language and indecent remarks and the situation got ugly.

"You recall Charlie Brown, from down at the saloon tonight? Well, he got wind of the problem and took a hand. When Rigney commenced to run his mouth again, Charlie hit him over the head with a pick handle and rendered him unconscious.

"Trouble is he rendered him *too* unconscious. They locked Rigney in a jail cell. When they came to take him out again, he was either dead or about to die. Some of the town's vigilante types were worried that Charlie would be charged with manslaughter or worse, so they took Rigney out and hung him from a railroad trestle. Whether he was alive or dead prior to the hanging nobody can say, but the townsfolk approved of Charlie's action and saved him from any possible trouble with the law."

Tom drank the last of his coffee and set the cup down on his desk. "It's a hell of a thing for a peace officer to say, but justice ain't always the same as law. Makin' trouble for a good man for *doin'* good just ain't in the public interest."

Two

THE MARK OF CAIN

I laid out my bedroll on the floor of Tom's office that night, but I can't say I slept much. Mostly, I tossed and turned like a tumbleweed in a gale, reliving every detail of the shooting. In memory, I saw Toby again on horseback, looking big as a skinned mule in his black hat and canvas duster.

Toby was dead within seconds. A quick search produced no gun belt, no gun, no weapon of any kind. And then I found not a gun, but a *harmonica!* I shot a boy whose "weapon" was meant only to kill lonesome, not men.

What could I have done differently? I could have waited; I could have held my fire. Yes, I thought, but what if Toby had been a hard case and a gunman? As Tom pointed out, I might well be dead myself.

I take my case to the judge in my mind. *I didn't know. It's not my fault.*

If that's so, the judge replies, *why do you feel so guilty?*

Morning dawned flat and gray under cloudy skies. I sat up in my blankets, as weary as when I laid down. Through the office window, the sun was a pale patch in the cloud cover, like a worn spot in a blanket. I donned my hat and pulled my britches on, looking out on a world as bleak as my mood.

I built a fire in the office stove and set the coffee pot on to boil. Washing up in cold water, I thought about Toby again. Toby would never feel cold, or warmth, or anything. Toby was dead and dead forever. In the mirror, my face looked sad and old; I did not recognize it as my own.

I pulled my boots on and picked up my gun belt. The forty-four seemed somehow heavier than before. *This is the gun that killed Toby Slocum,* I thought. "Death by misadventure," Tom had called it, an accident and nothing more. But I couldn't stop thinking about Toby.

It wasn't as if he was my first. I had killed men before—four in the line of duty and two before ever I wore a badge—nearly a man every year since 1882. I'd been shot three times myself, once above the hip, once in the back, and once in my right thigh. Deadly force was part of the job for a lawman, and would be as long as there were men who believed they could take what they wanted by force.

And yet the killing of Toby Slocum was different. I *felt* different. Picking up my cartridge belt, gun, and holster, I found I could not buckle them on. Something had changed in me. I wondered if I would ever be the same again.

• • •

I was waiting at the depot when the train pulled in. With a long, mournful wail of its whistle, the big 4-4-0 locomotive came barreling down the track past Fort Keogh, rolled across the Tongue River Bridge, and came chuffing to a stop at the station. I stood in the cold light of morning, watching the passengers step down and feeling as lonesome and lost as the steam whistle sounded.

There was no mistaking Chance Ridgeway for anyone else. Tall and lanky in his high-crowned Stetson and long black overcoat, the U.S. Marshal for Montana was a figure even school children recognized on sight. Now in his sixties, Ridgeway had become a legend for his dedication to the letter of the law. He had been my boss, adviser, and teacher for nearly five years, and he had made me his chief deputy. When he stepped off the train and smiled, I smiled back, but there was a lump in my throat the size of a door knob.

"Mornin', Chief," I said. "You're lookin' fit."

Ridgeway switched his Gladstone bag from his right hand to his left and we shook. I did my best to hide my feelings, but the marshal didn't miss much. I saw his gaze drop to my waist and note my missing revolver and then rise to meet my eyes again.

"I'm not in too bad a shape for the shape I'm in," he said. "These days, I'm mostly either tryin' to make water or remember somebody's name."

The MacQueen House stood just across the road from the depot. The rambling frame structure was to Miles City what the Cheyenne Club was to Cheyenne—a headquarters for cattlemen and high rollers, and the best hotel in town. Ridgeway regarded the building thoughtfully.

"I hear the MacQueen House boasts a new restaurant," Ridgeway said. "Let us go yonder and sample its wares. I'm buyin'."

My laugh was shaky. "I'm a little off my feed this mornin'," I said, "but I'll set with you while *you* eat. I need to talk some, Chief."

The marshal's glance was sharp. "Merlin Fanshaw not *hungry?* What is this world a-comin' to?"

I could not meet his eyes. "All right," he said. "We'll divide and conquer. I'll eat while you talk."

We entered the restaurant through a wide archway just off the hotel's lobby and were shown to a table by a young waiter who told us his name was Guilfoyle. At least a dozen tables filled the room, each with a spotless linen cloth and chairs that matched. Potted palms added a touch of greenery, and an open fire blazed in a huge stone fireplace. The place was mighty high-toned for a cow town eatery, but its charm was lost on me. My mind, as they say, was someplace else, and that someplace was gloomy and dark.

Guilfoyle handed a printed copy of the bill of fare to each of us, but I didn't look at mine. "Just coffee," I said. "If you please."

Squinting, Ridgeway studied the bill of fare at arm's length. The marshal wore spectacles for reading but when he was out in public he liked to pretend he didn't need them. I don't believe he fooled anybody.

"Bring me a ham steak," he told the waiter. "And two eggs on the sunny side. Add some fried spuds, a couple o' biscuits, and a pot of black coffee. Keep them eggs bright-eyed, Guilfoyle."

Guilfoyle smiled. "Very good, sir," he said, and headed back toward the kitchen.

Ridgeway fixed his ice-blue eyes on me. "All right, son," he said. "I'm listenin'."

My thoughts were as scattered as a trail herd after a cattle run. It took me a little time to round up the leaders and get them lined out again. I cleared my throat.

The words came, slow at first, and then like water through a broken dam. I told Ridgeway about the attempted robbery of the State National Bank and the killing of Toby Slocum, and I held nothing back.

Through it all, the marshal listened without comment. He waited until I had told it all and said, "A good report, Merlin. Sounds like you and Tom were alert and efficient. Too bad about the boy, but those things happen."

"You can *say* that, Chief. Far as I know, *you* never shot an unarmed child."

Ridgeway looked thoughtful. "No," he said. "Can't say as I ever did." Then, after a pause, he said, "I shot a *woman* once."

"A *woman!* How . . ."

"Back in Kansas it was. April of '78. I was workin' as a night deputy in Dodge City. A pair of drunken trail hands shot a bartender over at the Long Branch. When I showed up, they elected to make a fight, and the shootin' became general. After the smoke cleared, both men were down, but I found I'd also shot a dancehall girl name of Chastity Dupree.

"I felt mighty bad, but it was an accident, pure and simple. Not only had her parents gave Chastity the wrong name, the poor girl was unlucky. When the shootin' commenced she just happened to be standin' where the bullets went."

Guilfoyle brought our coffee to the table and poured us each a cup. Ridgeway took a sip of his, swallowed, and observed, "That's mighty good coffee." I sipped my own and thought it bitter as gall.

When the waiter had gone I said, "I can't stop thinkin' about that kid. He was simple of mind and gentle of spirit, and I shot him dead when he tried to show me his mouth harp. He was harmless as a dove, and I killed him."

Ridgeway nodded. "Yes, you did," he said.

"But you knew *none* of those things at the time. You had every reason to believe that boy was a bank robber, and a dangerous one to boot. You took the proper action, and you've no call to blame yourself."

"No matter how you cut it," I said, "I shot too quick and a boy is dead."

Ridgeway's voice was tight. "I've lost more than one deputy because he shot too *slow*."

At that point, Guilfoyle showed up with Ridgeway's breakfast and set it before him with a smile. Then he got a look at our faces. His smile faded and he turned away, heading back to the kitchen.

"That waiter must wonder who died," Ridgeway said.

"I could have *told* him," I said. "It was Toby Slocum."

We sat there for what seemed a long time. Ridgeway cleared his throat.

"You're a fine deputy," he said. "I would surely hate to lose you."

There was nothing more to say, and that was a good thing because I couldn't trust my voice right then anyway. All I knew was that I could no longer serve as a peace officer. Something inside me had broke and I didn't know how to fix it.

I unpinned the deputy's badge from my shirt and slid it across the tablecloth. The five-pointed star in a circle was a talisman between us. For a time, Ridgeway just looked at the badge. Then he said, "I'll keep this awhile. In case you change your mind."

I managed a smile. "Sure, chief," I said. "You do that."

Ridgeway's ham and eggs were growing cold. "What will you do, Merlin?" he asked. "Where will you go?"

"I don't know. Look for a ridin' job somewhere maybe. See some new country."

Ridgeway's smile was gentle. "Maybe, like Cain in the Bible, you'll go dwell in the land of Nod, on the east of Eden, and find yourself a wife."

"Could be," I said. "Now that I've learned I *am* my brother's keeper."

Back at Ringer and Johnson's, I paid the young hostler and picked up my horses. I saddled Rutherford and with the kid's help packed my bedroll on Roanie. Outside, the clouds had settled in, and the alkali buttes and sandstone bluffs beyond town were swallowed up and hidden behind the mist. With an eye on the weather, I loosed the saddle strings that held my slicker and shrugged into it.

The kid looked as though he thought I'd hung the moon, his manner respectful and polite. I gave him a closer look. "Do I know you?" I asked.

"Yes, sir," he said. "I'm Elroy Biggs. I met you

and Marshal Ridgeway three years back, here in Miles City."

"I remember," I said. "You're the boy who hankers to be a lawman some day."

"Yes, sir. The whole town's talkin' about the bank robbery last night. They say you shot Toby Slocum."

I felt like I'd been punched in the gut. I caught my breath and then let it out. "It was dark behind the bank," I said. "Toby was holdin' the horses. I thought he pulled a weapon."

"Nobody blames you, Deputy. They blame Toby's brothers for puttin' him at risk."

I took Rutherford's reins and set my foot in the stirrup. Holding the roan's lead rope in my left hand, I swung into the saddle. As I turned away, I looked back at Elroy. "You need to be careful about wantin' to be a lawman," I told him. "You just might get your *wish*."

The fog grew thicker as I rode away from Miles City, vapor rising from the dark waters of the Tongue and hiding the cottonwoods and willows along its banks. The trail I traveled was faint and grass-grown, but I gave Rutherford his head and allowed him to make his way as he would.

I was a stranger to myself. No longer a lawman, I was not sure *who* I was. For nearly five years, I had served as Chance Ridgeway's deputy. I had shared his vision and he had sold me on its worth. Together, we had stood between the decent folks and the outlaws. We carried justice in our hearts and on our hips. Doing good and righting wrongs had come to be my mission and my job.

And in those five years I *had* done some good. Maybe I'd even righted a wrong or two. I had walked through the valley of the shadow and had lived to see the light on the other side. I had held power over other men; power over their freedom and over their lives. When it had gone well, I'd known the quiet pride of a job well done and the satisfaction of having made a difference.

But now it had all gone wrong. I had lost the man I thought I was. My hope was that someday I might find him again.

During the next few days, I drifted with the wind by day, riding wherever the notion took me. I crossed Pumpkin Creek, Mizpah Creek, and a dozen little creeks I couldn't name. The range was mostly unsettled and open, and its vast grasslands, broken here and there by sandstone bluffs and round-topped buttes, seemed to go on forever. Pine-covered hills rose beneath a sapphire sky and cottonwood trees marked the course of sweet water streams. I saw cattle on the plains, elk and mule deer in the breaks, and pronghorn far out on the flats, but I saw only an occasional settler's cabin and no fences at all.

Come nightfall, I'd bed down on the banks of some small creek and set my horses out to graze.

34

There were road ranches along the Tongue where I might have stayed, but I wanted nothing of the company of men.

I had brought but few provisions when I'd come to Miles City and had purchased none while there. Come evening, I generally made a modest supper of bacon, and of hardtack so old and tough I had to soak it in my coffee before I could eat it. Rutherford and Roanie fared better than me; already, new grass grew along the creek banks and in the bottoms, and the ponies grazed in their hobbles without a care.

Come full dark, as my campfire died away to embers, I slipped between the soogans of my bedroll and gazed up at the stars. At a time when I was no longer sure of anything much, it was good to find that some things hadn't changed. Orion's Belt lit the southern skies as before. The Milky Way still paved what Indians call the Way of the Wolf with its broad and glittering trail. I laid there in my blankets until my eyes grew weary and took a notion of their own to close.

Then sleep came at last, even though I fought it for fear of meeting Toby Slocum in my dreams. As luck would have it, I never did. And that was a mercy, for I thought of him often enough by day.

I began to see more horses and cattle on the range, and from time to time a dirt-roofed cabin or two. I had run out of grub and coffee and was hungry as a wolf by that time. And even though I saw grouse and rabbits most every day that I could have killed with a six-gun, I did not. My .44 lay wrapped in its leather in my bedroll, but I couldn't bring myself to take it in hand. This led to some lively conversations with myself, as you might imagine.

What's the matter with you? Would you rather starve than shoot a durned rabbit?

It's not that I'd rather. I just can't take up a gun to kill even a critter.

If that's how it is, you better hope you don't run into a cranky rattlesnake.

If I do, I just hope the snake don't know how gun-shy I am.

I was having another of those conversations with myself one afternoon when I rode out atop a ridge and looked down on a rough-hewn cabin and a pole corral at the foot of the hill. A sorrel horse occupied the corral, and a saddled claybank stood ground-tied near the cabin door. Smoke drifted from a stovepipe at the cabin's north end, and the smell of cooking meat caught my full attention. I rode down the slope and drew rein.

"Hello the cabin!" I shouted.

A tall man appeared in the cabin's doorway. He was dressed for work on the range, from his high-crowned hat and shotgun chaps to his dusty boots, and he held a Colt's revolver in his right hand.

"What the hell do *you* want?" he asked.

RIDING THE GRUB LINE

The man in the doorway looked me over with narrowed eyes. I returned the favor, and took a closer look at *him*. He was middling tall, maybe five foot ten, and he appeared to be my age or a little older. He wore a faded flannel shirt beneath a woolen vest, and a black silk muffler was knotted loosely about his neck. His hair was black, too, and medium long. He wore his hat low and level above his eyes, and his face and hands were burned brown by the sun.

"I *asked* you what the hell you want," the tall man asked. "Are you deaf or just slow-witted?"

I smiled. "My name's Merlin Fanshaw," I said. "I won't beat around the bush, mister. I haven't et in a few days."

The tall man slid the gun back in the leather and stepped down from the door's threshold. "Ridin' the grub line," he snorted. "I might have known. You can't be all *that* hungry—you still have two fat horses."

"That just shows I take better care of my animals than I do myself," I said.

"All right," said the man. "Get down and come

inside. I've got venison cookin'. You're welcome to share it if you've a mind to."

I felt light-headed. I smiled a shaky smile. "I've a mind to," I said.

The line shack was fairly typical. Built of pine logs with the bark on and chinked with clay, the cabin was a no-frills home for a cow outfit's line rider, and that's what I judged the tall man to be. Hackamores, lead ropes, and a galvanized wash tub hung on nails against the cabin's outer wall and a water bucket and basin stood on a stand beside the doorway. I washed up, dried my face and hands with my bandanna, and stepped inside.

At first, I could make out but little of the cabin's interior. Coming into the cabin from the bright sunlight was like entering a coal mine. I stood, waiting until my eyes grew accustomed to the change. Slowly, details came into view—the ridge pole and rafters of pine, the overhead low. A floor of hard-packed dirt. The cabin, cluttered with all manner of pack saddles, panniers, manties, and rope. Crates nailed to the wall, serving as kitchen shelves. A rusted cook stove, leveled by flat rocks beneath its legs, a box for stove wood at its side. The tall man, filling his plate from a skillet and a Dutch oven. Homemade table and chairs fashioned from packing boxes and scrap lumber. A rope-strung bunk set against a side wall, the line rider's bedroll atop it.

The tall man turned away from the stove. He

handed me a heaping plate and a knife and fork. The plate held beans, sourdough biscuits, and a venison steak that hung over the plate's edges like a saddle blanket. "That mule deer meat's gettin' a little age on it," he said. "It's been hangin' for a week or two, but I don't reckon it'll kill us yet."

I took the plate. My hand trembled. The smell of those hot vittles nearly overcame me. "If it kills me," I said, "so be it."

He filled a plate for himself, and turned toward the door. "It's dark as a chippy's heart in here," he said. "Let's take this grub outside."

Sitting cross-legged on a plank that served as a front stoop, I tied into that chuck with a will. The tall man squatted beside me and we ate together in silence. I didn't think much about it at the time, but he'd dished up less food for himself than for me. I was still wolfing it down when he went back inside and came out with another steak, as big as the first. "You might as well eat this'n, too," he said. "I cooked too damn much meat, and I hate to throw it out."

By the time I finished that second steak, I felt better than I had in days. I also felt a bit stupefied, like a bull snake that had swallowed a rabbit. The tall man brought the coffee pot outside and refilled my cup. "I'm obliged to you, mister," I said. "This grub line ridin' ain't all it's cracked up to be."

"Don't 'mister' me, bub," he said. "My name is Hitch Holbrook."

I was feeling more pert with my belly full. "And don't *you* call me 'bub,'" I said. "I already *gave* you my name."

"Fanshaw, you said. Merlin Fanshaw."

I got to my feet. "That's right," I said. "Now that you've fed me, we need to go to the *other* part of ridin' the grub line, the part where I do some work to show my appreciation."

Hitch regarded me with that narrow-eyed squint he'd used when I first showed up. After a moment, he said, "Can you shoe a horse?"

"I can," I said.

Hitch nodded at the sorrel gelding inside the round corral. "That red horse is still wearin' heel corks from last winter," he said. "I need to pull those shoes and put flat plates on him."

"I'm your man," I said.

Hitch went back into the cabin and came out with a box containing shoes and shoeing tools. With me following in his footsteps, he led the way to the corral and opened the gate. We went inside and I closed the gate behind us.

While Hitch put a hackamore and lead rope on the sorrel, I took note of the tools—a shoeing hammer, nails, rasp, hoof knife, nipper, and a set of flat plates. Hitch put his hand on the sorrel's hip and crowded the animal over against the side of the corral, and I slipped the tools into the top of my boot, where they'd be handy.

"Been meanin' to shoe Old Red myself," Hitch said, "but ridin' line for the outfit don't leave a man much free time."

I picked up the sorrel's nigh hind foot and pulled the old shoe. Working on the hoof with knife and rasp, I soon had it ready for the new plates. "You say you ride for the outfit," I said. "What outfit would that be?"

Hitch fished a half-smoked stogie from a vest pocket and lit it. "Three C Bar," Hitch said. "Claymore Cattle Company, out of Glasgow, Scotland. There's a half-dozen outfits, big and small, runnin' cows and horses on this range."

I tapped a new shoe in place, and twisted off the nail's end. "I can see why," I said. "There's good grass, water, and open country as far as the eye can see."

Hitch nodded, looking off into the distance. He fell silent then, thinking his own thoughts, and I finished shoeing the sorrel. I straightened up and stretched, working the kinks out of my back, and put the tools back in the box.

"You *do* know how to shoe a horse," Hitch said. "You lookin' for work, or just passin' through?"

"Lookin' for a ridin' job," I said. "But so far, you're the first human I've seen."

"There are a few small outfits south and east of here, and one big spread, the Rafter D. Last I heard, the Rafter D had a full crew. They were even layin' men off."

"What about the small outfits?"

Hitch looked thoughtful. "The C Heart might be hirin'," he said. "Calvin Hart staked his claim back when this was Indian country. He passed away a few years ago, and his outfit has fell on hard times. The C Heart is a cow and calf outfit—they used to run better than six hundred pairs, but they're down to maybe half that number now. The home place is about ten miles from here as the crow flies. If the crow *walks*, it's more like *fourteen*."

Hitch nodded toward a long ridge off to the south. "There's an old wagon road on top o' that ridge," he said. "Goes right past the C Heart."

"How far to a town?" I asked.

"Town of Fairfax, fifteen miles beyond. A new burg, and still buildin'. The town dads cater to the big outfits and the money men behind 'em."

The sun was low on the horizon, and blue shadows had flowed down the hillsides and filled up the low places. Hitch scowled. "It's too late to ride out this evenin'," he said. "You might as well stay the night. I'll be headin' out myself before first light."

I nodded. "All right," I said. "I'll go take care of my horses."

I led Rutherford and Roanie down to the corral and took off their saddles and packs. Fifty yards from the cabin, a spring-fed stream flowed clear and cold, and I allowed both horses to drink their fill. By the time they finished, the sun had set, and the land gave up its color to the sky. Clouds went from gold to blood red, and faded quickly to gray. Off to the east, the first stars winked on. I picked up my horses' lead ropes and led them back down to the corral.

Hitch was there; he had turned his blue roan in with the sorrel, and the animals were nickering at each other and carrying on like long-lost friends. Hitch took the makings from his shirt pocket and rolled a cigarette. "Ponies sure are sociable," I remarked.

A match flared as Hitch lit his smoke. He dropped the match in the dirt of the corral and stepped on it. "A hell of a lot more so than *I* am," he said.

I rolled out my bed on the dirt floor of the line shack that night and crawled in. Out of habit, I found myself fighting sleep even though I was bone tired. Every night since the shooting at the bank, I'd feared the dreams that might haunt me— dreams of Toby Slocum, his life's blood flowing from his wounded breast and his eyes staring into mine. And always, in my imagination, he seemed to ask, "*Why?* Why did you *shoot* me?"

But on this night something changed. Maybe the need for sleep overcame my morbid fears, or maybe I just felt safe and welcome there in the line camp. Whatever the reason, I dropped off easy into a deep and dreamless sleep. That's all I recall until I woke up hours later to the smells of coffee and frying venison.

I sat up in my blankets and put my hat on. Hitch was already at the stove, and was cooking by lantern light. "About time you woke up," he said. "It's three-thirty in the mornin', and we're burnin' daylight."

I didn't argue. I was glad to wake up rested, and I was in an agreeable state of mind.

"Same song, second verse," Hitch said. "Risky deer meat and two-day-old beans—get 'em while they're hot."

We ate quickly. I washed our dishes in a battered dishpan and set them on the table to dry. Then we saddled up down at the corral and Hitch helped me pack my bed on Roanie. Leading our horses back up to the line shack, Hitch held out his hand. "Luck to you, Merlin," he said.

I took his hand. "Obliged."

His smile was a quick flash. Stepping up into the saddle, he sank spur and rode away into the darkness.

Frost rimed the bunch grass and lay white along the bottoms as I took my horses through the broken country that led to the ridge. The skin of my face and hands tightened with the chill of our passing, and my breath exploded in puffs of vapor-like smoke from pistol shots. Juniper and scrub pine swept past, and I flushed a group of whitetail deer in the semi-darkness. They bounded away like ghosts, their tails white flags in the gloom.

Overhead, stars grew dim and vanished as darkness faded into daylight. I turned the horses up the slope that led to the crest of the ridge and heard them labor, breathing hard, rocks clattering beneath their hooves as they lunged to the top.

And then I broke out into sunlight, the bunch grass and the sage atop the ridge washed in brightness, and the wagon road laid out before me. I drew rein and stepped down to let the horses blow and to check their cinches. Turning my back to the east, I saw my shadow cast sixty yards and more beyond me. From the ridgetop, the land seemed to have no limit, pine-covered hills and rolling plains stretching all the way to the distant mountains. It was a good day to be alive.

As the day wore on, I began to see more cattle on the plains. Twice, I stopped to study the country through my old Army field glasses, and was surprised to see mostly cattle of the Shorthorn and Durham breeds instead of the multi-colored Texas Longhorns I was accustomed to. I saw only an occasional settler's cabin and no people at all. The big open country seemed to belong entirely to livestock and wildlife.

Then, about mid-afternoon, I caught sight of

log buildings in a clearing just below the ridge. Big cottonwood trees stood tall along a creek that flowed through the barn lot, and I saw a modest ranch house and outbuildings, including a bunkhouse, stable, and barn. A fenced stock pen opened off the barn, and a round corral for working broncs stood apart, near the creek. There were horses in the corral, and smoke drifted up from a stovepipe at the main house. The distance from the line shack had been fourteen miles, or close to it. From what Hitch had said, I figured I was looking at the C Heart ranch headquarters.

Turning the horses down off the ridge, I rode up to the main house and drew rein. Built of log, like the other buildings, the house faced east and featured a screen porch and a front yard enclosed by a whitewashed rail fence. A raised boardwalk formed a pathway above the mud that led from the gate to the front door. I waited for a time, but it appeared no one was home.

I was about to ride on when a woman opened the front door and stepped outside. I'm no hand at guessing a woman's age, but I'd say she was somewhere in her mid-forties. She wore a man's old sheepskin coat over a house dress and apron. Shading her eyes against the sun, she looked up at me.

"Can I help you?" she asked. Her voice had a husky, lived-in tone.

I took my hat off and smiled. "Yes'm," I said. "Lookin' for the owner."

The woman returned my smile. My first thought was that she was plain-featured, homely even. Her face was deeply wrinkled, and her skin sunburned and brown as an old saddle. But her eyes were clear and startlingly blue. Laugh lines at the corners of her eyes and mouth spoke of good humor and disposition. "Owner left for the north pasture an hour ago," she said. "Seems an early calf is comin' into the world, and its mother needs a little help. Or a *lot* of help, more likely."

"I'd be happy to lend a hand," I said. "How would I find the north pasture?"

She pointed to a bridge across the creek beyond the barn. "Across that bridge and maybe two miles along the base of those hills."

"All right if I leave my packhorse here?"

She nodded. "Certainly. Just tie him over at the corral."

Leaving Roanie at the corral, I rode Rutherford across the barn lot at a brisk, go-to-work trot. The bridge planks rumbled hollow beneath me as I crossed the creek, and then I was riding fast along a road that skirted the sagebrush-covered hills north of the ranch. Open pasture land lay between the hills and the creek, and I saw a score of Durham heifers as I rode.

Maybe a mile and a half further, I came around a bend in the road and saw two saddled horses standing ground-tied near a brushy patch by the creek. Thirty feet away lay a heifer in labor and in trouble. Two ranch hands squatted in the mud nearby, trying to help, but they didn't seem to be having much luck. The heifer lay heavy on her side, her belly huge and bulging. From time to time she seemed to stiffen, thrashing and kicking, and tossing her head.

The heifer rolled her eyes and bawled a moaning, coughing sound that spoke clearly of her misery and pain. From the marks in the soft ground, she'd been in hard labor for some time, and she was nearly at the end of her rope.

I guess I was concentrating on the heifer. I hadn't really taken note of the people who were trying to help her. I took a closer look, and was surprised by what I saw. One of the riders was a *girl!* At least, that was my first impression. On closer inspection she turned out to be a pretty young woman in men's work clothes. A well-seasoned *sombrero* sat low above her wide brown eyes. Her hair was a honeybrown color, pulled straight back and fashioned in a single braid at the back of her head. Her face was sober, her expression one of concern.

The other rider was an older man with a wispy walrus mustache. He knelt at the heifer's hind-quarters, the sleeve of his flannel shirt rolled to the shoulder and his arm fish-belly white and slick with the heifer's fluids. He was a sun-dried, wizened gent with faded blue eyes, and he seemed startled to see me. I guessed him to be the owner of the C Heart.

"Can I help?" I asked.

"Her calf is breeched," the old man said. "I tried to turn it, but I don't have the strength."

"I'll try," I said. I took off my coat and my shirt, and knelt beside the man. Thrusting my arm deep into the hot wetness of the heifer's vagina, I found the old man was right; the calf was indeed turned, and in the breech position. Carefully feeling my way, I found the calf's forelegs and slowly worked to turn it the other way.

It was hard to keep a firm grip, and harder still to turn the calf, but with considerable effort I finally got the little feller headed right. The heifer tried to push her baby out, but she was weak from her long struggle. I pulled, my hands aching and my arms and shoulders cramping, and drew the calf's soft, pink hooves out through the vaginal opening. Then the head and shoulders appeared. I gave one hard last pull, the heifer strained again, and the calf slid out slicker than an otter down a creek bank.

The woman's face brightened. She smiled at the wet, sticky newborn and wiped its nostrils with her gloved hand. The heifer got her hind legs under her, and struggled to a standing position. I straddled the calf and lifted it to its feet, where it stood, wobbly and shivering, at its mother's side.

I walked down to the creek and washed off the blood and afterbirth in the icy water. I used my shirt to dry my hands and arms and then put it on again and buttoned it. By the time I got back the old man and the woman were watching the heifer nuzzle her calf, and were smiling all around. The woman turned to me. "Much obliged for your help," she said. "I'm glad you happened by."

"Likewise," said the old man. "I ain't much of a midwife these days."

"To tell the truth, I wasn't just passin' by," I said. "I was lookin' to talk to you, if you're the owner of the outfit."

The old man laughed. "You're barkin' up the wrong tree, son," he said. "*I* ain't the owner . . ."

He nodded at the woman. ". . . *She* is."

The woman met my eyes and smiled. "Billie Hart," she said. "Welcome to the C Heart."

TO RIDE FOR THE C HEART

I was caught off guard. I had assumed the old man must own the C Heart ranch. Instead, the owner turned out to be a pretty young woman named Billie Hart. I doffed my hat and stammered. "Sorry, ma'am . . . *miss*. I-I thought . . ."

"You thought Clem here must be the boss rancher because he's a man. A natural mistake. *Everybody* knows only a *man* can run a cow outfit, right?"

"*Yes,* ma'am . . . I mean *no,* miss! I reckon a woman can do most anything a *man* can. I only . . ."

Billie's laughter was like music. "Relax, cowboy," she said. "I'm just having a little fun at your expense." She offered her hand, and I took it. "Call me Billie. You said you came here to see me?"

"Yes, ma'am . . . I mean yes, *Billie*. My name's Merlin Fanshaw. I'm lookin' for work. I wondered if the C Heart could use another hand."

Billie looked at me straight on and level, as if I was a horse she was thinking of buying.

"Where have you worked, Merlin?"

"Thane McAllister's M Cross, over in Progress County. Here and there."

"Must have been a while back," she said. "You have soft hands for a working cowboy."

I met her gaze. "It's been awhile," I said. "But I'll make you a good hand."

She didn't reply, but kept her eyes locked on mine. I didn't look away.

Billie turned to the old man. "What do you think, Clem? Should we hire this drifter?"

The man's laugh was a high-pitched cackle. "Hell, Billie," he said. "He already saved you one good cow and a calf."

He turned to me. "I'm Clem Guthrie," he said. "I've knowed Billie since she wore three-cornered pants and ate dirt. You'll never work for a better boss."

Billie smiled. "I guess that settles it," she said. "Clem's about half worthless these days, but he's a good judge of whiskey and men. Looks like you're riding for the C Heart, Merlin."

We caught up our horses and headed back to the home ranch. Billie rode beside me, and Clem brought up the rear. Now that I was on the payroll, I took a closer look at the meadows and fenced pasture that helped to make up the outfit. I liked what I saw.

"The C Heart is sort of a shirt-tail ranch these days," Billie said, "but it's still a nice little spread. We run about three hundred pairs now, mostly on open range, but we winter them here on the home place."

"Tell him about the 'soup kitchen'," Clem said.

Billie's face softened. "Calvin Hart, my dad, was a good cow man, but he was something of a dreamer," she said. "Dad heard about Colonel Drake's petroleum discoveries back in Pennsylvania, and decided he'd look for his own 'black gold' here on the ranch. Hired a prospector with a drilling rig, and sank two wells. First well was a dry hole, but the second . . .

"Well, Dad didn't strike oil with the second well, but he hit something almost as rare, especially in *this* country—an *artesian well!* Soft as rain, the water comes out of the wellhead at ninety degrees Fahrenheit and ninety pounds pressure!"

Clem Guthrie moved up beside us. Laughing, and excited by the memory, he interrupted Billie's story. "That's a fact!" he said. "That durned Cal piped water over to the main house, and built a bath house right at the well! And then he put in a big galvanized stock tank down at the barn lot—watered his cows in the wintertime with *hot water!* Called it his 'soup kitchen'!"

Billie laughed, too—an honest, open laugh. "A few of our neighbors sank wells," she said, "hoping they'd hit artesian water, too. No one did."

"So you have the only 'soup kitchen' in these parts," I said. "That has to give you an edge when it comes to gettin' your stock through the winter."

"It does," Billie said, "And when I was a skinny kid in pigtails, I learned to *swim* in that tank."

We pulled up at the main house, and Billie stepped down. Handing Clem her horse's reins, she looked up at me. "Roll out your bed and stow your possibles at the bunkhouse," she said. "Clem will show you where. Supper back here at the house in half an hour."

"Yes, ma'am," I said.

Billie gave me a sharp glance, but her smile took the edge off. "From this point on," she said, "every time you call me 'ma'am,' I'll dock your pay a dollar."

My ears burned, and I knew I was blushing. "Sorry," I said. "I tend to be a slow learner sometimes . . . *Billie*."

"Me, too," she said, laughing. "And every time I forget *your* name, I'll *pay* you a dollar." Then she turned and entered the house.

Clem grinned at me. "Ain't she a *pistol?*" he asked. "The boss lady does like to *test* a man." Leading Billie's horse, he turned his own mount toward the barn.

I met Clem's grin with my own. I found I was still flustered by Billie's teasing. "She does have a way of keepin' a man off balance," I said.

Down at the barn, Clem helped me unpack Roanie and showed me where to stow my pack saddle and panniers. I unsaddled Rutherford, and gave both horses a good rubdown before leading them into an empty stall. Clem forked a few flakes of hay into the manger and then led the way to the bunkhouse, while I hefted my bedroll and wished it weighed less.

The C Heart bunkhouse sat back in the trees, not far from the barn. Built of log and set on a rock foundation, the building boasted a raised veranda, shaded by a board-and-batten awning. Inside, four double-decker bunks provided sleeping space for eight men. At the room's center, a rusted Sunshine stove promised warmth on a cold night. Beside the door, a rickety wash stand held a water bucket and basin. A flour sack that served as a towel hung from a nail below a cracked mirror. At the room's only window, a battered table held a coal-oil lamp, a greasy deck of playing cards, and a battered cribbage board.

"All the comforts of home," I said. "I expect there's a hooter out back."

"Fifty yards to the south," Clem said. "A one-holer."

Clem walked to the only bunk that held a bedroll and put his hand on it. "This'n is mine," he said. "You're plumb welcome to any other'n."

I hefted my roll. "I'll take that lower bunk, nearest the door," I said. As I turned toward the bunk I noticed another range bed, spooled and tied with rope, on the floor near the wash stand.

"Whose bed is that?" I asked.

Clem snorted. "Kid Billie hired name of Kip Merriday. Mean little bastard. Full of himself, and pushy. Billie thinks some C Heart cows and calves may have strayed. She sent Merriday out to haze 'em back this way."

"And Merriday didn't even take time to roll out his bed?"

"I *said* he was pushy. Packs a fancy nickel-plated six-shooter, and seems to think he's some kind of gunfighter. When he got mouthy with me I told him I'd wait 'til he was asleep some night and break his durned legs with a sledge hammer."

I laughed. "You're about half pushy *yourself*," I said. "How did Merriday take that?"

"Oh, he stayed snotty and mean, but I'd gave him somethin' to think about. He set his bedroll down there and slunk off like a barkin' dog. I haven't seen him since."

The clanging of a ranch triangle broke the stillness. "First call to supper," Clem said.

"I'm ready," I said, and we stepped out into the twilight.

When Clem and me entered the kitchen, I saw Billie Hart seated at the head of a long table drinking coffee. The woman I spoke to when I first rode in smiled from her place at the stove, her hair disheveled and her cheeks flushed from the heat.

"Welcome to the C Heart, cowboy," she said.

"We met earlier today, but we didn't trade names. I'm Maggie Adair, chief cook and bottle washer for this outfit."

"And the best friend I ever had," Billie said. "Maggie, meet Merlin Fanshaw. He saved a cow and a calf for us today, and hit me up for a job. So I hired him, on the condition he saves a cow and a calf for us *every* day."

Maggie smiled. "Good to meet you, Merlin. I don't believe we ever *had* a bona fide *cow savior* on the place before."

I was pleased by all this affable banter, but I didn't know how to answer it. I just grinned and maybe blushed a little, hoping that might pass for my good-natured participation. The ladies' joshing had thrown me off balance, and Clem was enjoying my discomfort. Too durned *much,* in my opinion.

The table was set for three, and Maggie brought a platter of roast beef, boiled spuds, carrots, and onions and set it before us. "Eat hearty, boys," Billie said. "Kip just rode in, but we won't wait for him. He'll be along when he's ready."

Maggie filled our cups from the coffee pot and sat down with a cup of her own. "You gentlemen go ahead," she said. "I'll eat later, with Billie."

She didn't have to tell me twice. The smell of Maggie's cooking had captured my full attention the minute I stepped through the doorway, and I wasn't slow in showing my appreciation.

We were just finishing up when I heard the front door open and close again, I heard stomping and shuffling in the entry way, and then Kip Merriday came up the steps. He took his hat off and tossed it in the corner, greeting Billie with a nod. "Sorry I'm late, Billie," he said. "I've put in a long day."

Something in his tone of voice made it sound like *he'd* been working, but we *hadn't*. I decided Clem's description of the man was pretty close to accurate. I studied him over the rim of my coffee cup, gathering my own information.

Merriday was maybe eighteen or nineteen. He was fair-haired and pink-skinned, like General Custer, with cold blue eyes and a three-hair mustache. Fancy garters held his shirtsleeves up, and the nickel-plated six-shooter Clem described hung low at his waist. He sized me up with a hard glance that told me I didn't impress him much. He swung his legs over the bench and sat down across from Clem and me. "I didn't know you were hirin' more help, Billie," he said.

"I didn't either," Billie said, "but I can always use a good man."

Then, quietly, she said, "Hang your gun out in the entry hall, Kip. I don't allow weapons at my table."

Sudden anger flashed in Kip's eyes, but he quickly replaced it with a smile. "Sure, Billie," he said. "This old hogleg is such a part of me I plumb forgot I had it on."

He stood, unbuckling the gun belt, and stepped out into the entry way. Seconds later, he was back at the table, without his fancy firearm. He helped himself to the beef, and looked me over like he smelled something bad. "Does this 'good man' have a name?" he asked. "Mine's Merriday. Kip Merriday."

I put my coffee cup down. "You say your name like you think I should know it. I don't. I'm Merlin Fanshaw."

I offered him my hand across the table, and he took it. We had howdied and shook, but that didn't make us friends.

Billie caught Merriday's eye. "What about your circle this morning? Did you find any C Heart stock?"

Merriday shook his head. "Nope," he said. "I saw cattle with half a dozen different brands, but not a single C Heart cow."

Billie frowned. "We're missing forty pairs—cows and calves—maybe more. They have to be somewhere."

She stared into her coffee cup. For a long moment she was silent. Then she raised her head and looked first at me and then at Merriday. She said, "I'd like you and Merlin to comb that country between Powder River and Mizpah Creek," she said. "If our cattle drifted, they likely wound up down along the creek bottoms."

Billie looked at me. "Merlin, I want you to take

the east side of the Powder and ride north to where the Mizpah joins it," she said. "You're new to this range, but I'll draw you a good map."

She turned to Merriday. "And Kip, you do the same. I want you to ride the *west* side. If our cattle crossed the river, I expect they'll be somewhere between the Powder and Mizpah Creek."

"What about calving here at the ranch?" I asked.

"Clem and I can handle it," Billie said. "I want you and Kip to get an early start. Breakfast at four-thirty."

The clouds still held traces of color as I walked with Clem back to the bunkhouse, but dusk was coming on fast. Here and there, stars glittered in the darkening sky, and the songbirds fell silent. We stepped up onto the bunkhouse veranda, and I stood still for a moment, just listening to the quiet.

"You fixin' to ride a horse from Billie's string in the mornin'?" Clem asked.

"I'll ride my own," I said. "My horse Roanie needs the work."

"It's your call. Billie has a pretty good cavvy for a spread this size."

"I don't doubt it. I'll get acquainted with the C Heart cavvy soon, but for now I'll go with a horse I know."

Inside, Clem struck a match and lit the lamp. I heard footfall on the veranda, and Kip Merriday swaggered through the doorway. His right hand hung near the pearl-handled revolver on his hip, his fingers opening and closing nervously. The kid's hard gaze bounced from Clem to me and back again in what I reckon was meant to be a menacing glare. I wasn't impressed. He looked for all the world like a ruffled banty rooster posing as a fighting cock.

His glance came to rest on my bedroll. "I see you put your damn bedroll on my *bunk,*" he said. I turned, looking at the bunk and then back at Merriday.

"No," I said. "I put it on *my* bunk."

"You're a damned *liar!*" he said. "I claimed that bunk the day I signed on."

"Then you should have put your bed on it." I made a sweeping gesture with my hand that took in the entire bunkhouse. "There are six empty bunks in here, kid," I said. "Choose any, or all."

Merriday's eyes flashed. He took a quick stride forward, his hand reaching toward my bunk. I stepped in front of him, blocking his path. "Touch my bed, and you'll be ridin' circle tomorrow with a broken arm," I said.

He hesitated, but he wasn't ready to back off. His shoulder dropped, and I saw the sucker punch coming even before it was fully formed. Blocking his blow with my left arm, I slapped him hard across the face with my open hand. Merriday lost his hat; he stumbled and nearly fell. His blue eyes lost their focus, and the skin of his face blazed red where I'd hit him.

"Behave youself," I said.

Merriday's fingers closed on the grips of his revolver, jerking it part way from its holster. My own hand flashed to my hip; I recalled that I no longer went heeled. I crouched, facing the kid. Hot anger caught in my throat and made my voice tight. "Go ahead," I said. "Pull that pimp's pistol and I'll make it part of your body."

The kid had made his play, but the results had surprised him. I watched his face, saw doubt struggle against bluster. A thin trickle of blood crept down from a nostril and stained his future mustache. I had called his bluff. I had hurt his pride. I locked my eyes on his, and waited.

"Well?" I said. "Are you goin' to pull that gun, or pull your *freight?*"

Merriday had lost most of his swagger. He pushed the revolver back in its leather and took his hand away.

"Hell," he said. "You ain't *worth* killin'. There'll be another time."

"Somehow I don't think so," I said. "I'd like to believe you're smarter than that."

Merriday picked up his bedroll and carried it to an empty bunk at the far end of the room. That

was all right with me. The farther the better, I thought.

Clem Guthrie shucked his britches and turned down the blankets on his bed. Stepping over to the table, he cupped his hand above the lamp chimney and gave me a thoughtful look. Then he blew out the light, and the room went dark. But just before it did, I had a clear look at Clem's face. His eyes were bright in the lamplight, and he wasn't smiling exactly, but he sure was trying hard *not* to.

Five

RUMORS OF RUSTLERS

I awoke in full darkness, and did not at first know where I was. Then the familiar smells of old leather, wet wool, and horse sweat jogged my memory, and I began to recall the events of the previous day. The bunkhouse at the C Heart ranch. Clem Guthrie. Kip Merriday. Billie Hart's warm brown eyes at the supper table, and her words.

We're missing forty pairs, or better. They have to be someplace.

I want you and Kip to get an early start.

Breakfast at four-thirty.

Kip. Kip Merriday. One more cocky kid, trying to hide his self doubt behind a smart mouth and an attitude. Full of bluster and beans, like many another young buck. Like I once was myself.

I heard the rustle of a bed tarp thrown back, feet scuffling in the gloom. Then a sulfur match, bursting into flame, and I saw Clem Guthrie lighting the lamp on the table by the window.

"Roll out, boys," he said. "It's daylight in the canyon."

"Maybe *someplace* in the world," I said. "but it sure ain't *here*."

Clem pulled on a pair of well-worn woolen pants and reached for his boots. "Dam' if I know why *I'm* gettin' up," he said. "It's you and Merriday have to comb the Big Open for strays."

I looked at my pa's old silver watch by the light of the oil lamp. "It's only a little past four," I said. "Time enough to groom old Roanie and put a saddle on him."

From the far end of the bunkhouse, I heard Merriday say, "I got *my* horse in last night. Top hands always get ready for work the night before."

"So I understand," I replied, "but I can't do that with my Roanie horse. He's a card-carryin' member of the saddle horse union, and he's not *allowed* to get ready until the actual work day."

Clem struggled to keep a straight face. "That's right," he told Merriday. "You're lucky your hoss is non-union."

Merriday gave me a befuddled look as I walked outside and made my way toward the barn. He may have had a sense of humor, but if so I hadn't seen it yet.

Roanie stood in the big corral behind the barn with my Rutherford horse and a half dozen C Heart horses, but he broke away from the bunch and trotted over to me when I stepped through the gate. I led the big roan inside and poured him a scoop of oats while I curried him, then I slipped

my saddle onto his withers and left him loose-cinched in his stall to finish his breakfast.

Lamplight glowed warm through the kitchen windows as I approached the house. Ahead of me, Clem Guthrie walked the raised planks that served as Billie's sidewalk, his arms out for balance like a tightrope walker. A dozen paces to the rear, Kip Merriday followed, strutting across the muddy barn lot. I shook my head. It takes a certain *style* to be able to strut through cold mud.

Billie—or Maggie, more likely—had provided a boot jack in the entryway at the house, and Clem and Kip had already shucked their boots when I walked through the door. I smiled as I saw that Kip had hung his gun and cartridge belt on a peg, this time without Billie telling him to. I thought, *Maybe the kid is a learner, after all.*

The warmth of the kitchen and the good smells of bacon, hotcakes, and coffee were maybe simple pleasures, but they made a man look forward to his work day, at least they did me. Maggie flipped hotcakes on a griddle, turning from her work to give me a quick smile. Billie sat at her usual place at the table's head, a steaming mug of coffee in her small hands, and she greeted me with a smile of her own.

"Sit down, Merlin," she said. "I expect you and Kip to eat a healthy breakfast this morning. We don't want Maggie to think you don't like her cooking."

"That would *never* do," I said. "I promise to consume her cooking in huge quantities, and with great enthusiasm. Compared to me, Maggie will consider a timber wolf to be a picky eater."

Having made my boast, I did my best to live up to it. Maggie's breakfast was larruping, and I went back for seconds, which seemed to please her to no end. And when it came to putting away grub, Kip Merriday kept up with me just fine. Of course, he was a youth in his teens; when I was his age, you couldn't have filled me up with a scoop shovel.

We didn't linger long at the table; Kip and me had miles to cover that day and I was eager to get horseback and out on the range. But even as we stood up from the table, Maggie insisted on sending leftover hotcakes with us for our noon meal. She gave us each a good portion of cakes, wrapped in a tea towel, and an airtight of tomatoes to boot.

Billie offered us both a map of the country we were to cover, and I was glad to have it. Kip said he didn't need a map because he was part Indian and had this mysterious natural gift for understanding new country. I took his claim not with a grain of salt, but with a whole durned *sack* of it. The only natural gift I'd seen Kip Merriday exhibit was being obnoxious.

False dawn was coming on as we led our ponies out of the barn and untracked them. We gave them each their fill of water at the creek, and then

we set foot in the stirrup, sunk spur, and lit out on our cow hunt.

For the first five miles or so, I rode with Kip across the rolling country that led to Powder River. Round-topped buttes lay shadowed at the prairie's edge like sleeping buffalo, and coming daylight erased the stars. Born of the morning, a fresh breeze ruffled the grasses and sighed through the sagebrush.

Roanie carried me along at a steady trot, his ears and eyes busy with the sight of new country. The big roan was not as clear footed or steady as my buckskin, but he was eager to learn, and he answered well to both rein and spur.

Sunlight broke above the far mountains and painted the hilltops. In that fragile month of May, the country was as rich and verdant as it would be all year, and new grass stood tender green all across the plains. Ahead, the Powder River reflected color to the sky and meandered, shallow and wide, along its border of cottonwood trees. Merriday pulled up at the river's edge and twisted in his saddle to look at me.

"Well, here's where we split up," he said. "Now if you lose your map, old-timer, just send up a prayer and suck your thumb. I'll come and lead you back to the home place."

"Don't fall off while you're crossin' the river," I advised. "That fancy pistol you carry will sink you like a stone."

Merriday answered me with a sneer and a cuss word, and rode his horse off into the muddy waters of the Powder. As I watched him cross the river, it occurred to me I'd likely have to give him another lesson in manners sometime, but the morning was bright as birdsong and I felt too good to let one lippy kid ruin my day.

I spent most of that morning following the river bank. From time to time, I'd ride Roanie up a hill and scan the area below with my field glasses. Twice, I ran across small bunches of cattle, but none of them were C Heart stock. Aside from a scatter of antelope out on the plains, nothing seemed to be moving in all that open country.

The day grew warm. Around noon, I took Roanie up a pine-topped hill and allowed him to graze in his hobbles while I made a meal of Maggie's pancakes and the can of tomatoes she sent. I carried no canteen, and the top of that hill was dry as a lizard's breath, so the juice from those canned tomatoes was especially welcome.

I took the hobbles off Roanie and was about to get horseback again when I saw maybe a dozen pairs, cows and calves, far out on the flat to the east. Thinking I'd found some of the missing C Heart stock, I put the roan into a trot and rode on down there. When I got close enough to read their brands, I saw that the cows wore the Rafter D brand. I turned away, and was about to continue

upriver when three men on horseback rode up out of a dry wash and blocked my path. I drew rein and faced them.

The riders watched me intently, easing their horses up the hill. They fanned out as they drew near, one man to my left, one to my right, and the third man facing me directly. Each man wore a belted revolver, and carried a Winchester repeating rifle in a saddle scabbard. *These boys are loaded for bear,* I thought.

The man who faced me reined up and rested his hands on his saddle horn. He was a good-looking gent in his mid- to late forties, his skin brown from the sun, and clean-shaven except for a thin black mustache. Beneath a high-crowned Stetson, his hair was black as well, going to gray at the temples.

"Morning," he said.

I glanced at the other riders. The man to my right was younger, maybe thirty. He was a beefy man with red hair and a fighter's nose. He stared coolly at me from the saddle, his face bland and without expression.

The third man was wiry and lean, with cold gray eyes in a pockmarked face. He wore a black, Navajo style hat, and his hair was chalk white, hanging loose and lank down to his shoulders. *Gun hand,* I thought.

I turned back to the man who faced me. "Mornin'," I replied.

"I'm Ross Devlin," the man said. "I own the Rafter D, east of here."

He leaned over the pommel of his saddle, looking at Roanie's shoulder brand, MF connected. The rider straightened, met my eyes. "I know most of the horse brands here in the Big Open," he said, "but I'm afraid I don't know that one."

"I'm new hereabouts," I said. "That's a Progress County brand."

Devlin kept his voice friendly, but his eyes went hard. "I just gave you *my* name. Mind giving me *yours?*"

"Fanshaw," I said. "Merlin Fanshaw. I ride for the C Heart."

Devlin's eyes widened slightly. "I know the C Heart well," he said. "I talked to Billie Hart three days ago in Fairfax. She said nothing about taking on another cow hand."

"That was three days ago," I said. "Billie hired me yesterday."

Devlin seemed to weigh my words. "Mind telling me what you're doing here?"

I was getting tired of the man's questions. Asking a man's name, or his occupation, was considered bad manners, at best, on the open range.

"I'd have to say that's none of your *business*, Mister Devlin."

Anger flashed in Devlin's eyes. He flushed, his

jaw muscles tense. I watched as he drew a check rein on his temper. When he spoke again, his voice was level, controlled.

"You're right, cowboy. I meant no offense. The fact is the Rafter D and several other outfits hereabouts have been losing livestock this spring. To *rustlers,* we believe. Stock thieves are *every* honest man's business, wouldn't you say?"

That explains the gun hand, I thought.

I nodded. "Yes, I would. The C Heart is missing maybe forty pairs. Billie sent me and another man out to look for them."

"Yes," Devlin said. "They could be *lost,* they could have *strayed.* And they could be . . ."

I finished his sentence. *". . . stolen,"* I said.

Devlin turned his horse away. "Yes," he said. "Tell Billie I'll keep an eye out for her cows. We'll let her know if we run across them."

"I will," I said. "Much obliged."

"Not at all. Billie's an old friend."

Devlin and the other two men turned their horses away and rode down the slope. I watched until they reached the plain above the river and turned east. Within minutes, they were lost to sight. Then I rode Roanie north to where Mizpah Creek joined the Powder, but I didn't turn up a single C Heart cow.

On my way back to the ranch that afternoon, I paid particular attention to the cottonwood groves and willows along the river's banks. The under-

growth was thick in places, and I figured cattle could well be hidden back in the trees. I suppose it was a good idea to search there, but my efforts turned up only a few deer and clouds of mosquitoes—to Roanie's dismay, and my own.

What Devlin had said about rustlers got me to thinking, and I began to keep an eye out for all the places where outlaws might hold stolen stock, work brands, and such. The range was vast, with most every kind of terrain a man could think of. There were pine-studded hills, bunch grass plains, and rich bottom land along the river. There were washouts and coulees and alkali flats as white as snow. And there were hidden canyons and badlands, choked with diamond willow and buffalo berry thickets, where a man could hold and hide a fair-sized herd. For the rest of that day I made a search of every coulee, draw, and box canyon I came across, but I turned up no trace of the C Heart cattle.

The sun was an orange ball above the distant mountains as I turned Roanie back toward the home place. Shadows crept into the hollows, and sunlight glowed warm across the plains and hillsides. I had gathered no cattle, so I gathered my thoughts instead.

I had turned in my badge and put away my gun. I had resigned—Ridgeway might say I had *deserted*—the law and order trade, because it *cost* too much. I had killed an unarmed boy and had

made him immortal, for he would live as long as *I* did in my mind and heart.

Looking for a new life, I had found one at the C Heart. But now rumors of rustlers had come, like clouds that block the sun and threaten stormy weather. Surely, I said to myself, there must be a place *somewhere* that's free of lawbreakers and violence.

And then, the answer came. If there is such a place, it has no people, for we *all* hold darkness in our hearts.

The hour was late when I got back to the ranch. Down at the horse corral, Kip Merriday's sorrel lifted its head and whinnied, asking Roanie what had kept him, I suppose. Back in the trees, lamplight glowed in the bunkhouse window. I was hungry. Kip and Clem had no doubt had their suppers and were settled in for the night while I was just getting back. All in a day's riding, I thought.

I led Roanie into a barn stall and poured a can of oats in his feed box. While the big horse ate, I stripped my saddle and blankets from his back and wiped him down with a grain sack. Then I forked some hay into the manger and walked across the lot to the main house.

Inside, Billie was waiting. She stood up and smiled as I came in. "Evening, Merlin," she said. "Sit down. Supper's in the oven."

Warmed by the cook stove, the kitchen was a

haven from the cold. Billie poured me a cup of coffee and freshened her own. There were questions in her eyes.

"No luck, Billie," I said. "I rode to the junction of Mizpah and the Powder and back through the trees along the river. No sign of any C Heart stock."

Disappointment passed over Billie's face like cloud shadow crossing a meadow. "Too bad," she said. "I was hoping you'd have better luck."

"I was, too," I said. "How did Kip make out?"

"The same. No C Heart cattle."

Billie filled a plate from the roasting pan and set it before me. The smells of beef, spuds, carrots, and gravy reminded me just how hungry I was. As I tied into my supper, Billie sat quietly with her coffee, watching me. There were still questions in her eyes but she seemed content to wait for their answers. Neither of us spoke but I found myself glancing at her now and then as I ate. Each time I did, I found her watching me with a level, straight gaze, open and unflinching. I had not known all that many women in my life, but even so, I don't recall any who looked at a man the way Billie did.

I finished my supper and pushed the plate away. "There is something else," I said. "Three men rode out of a dry wash about midday and braced me. They seemed mighty interested in who I was and what I was doing."

Billie waited for the rest of it.

"Man I spoke to said he's an old friend of yours. Said his name is Ross Devlin and that he owns the Rafter D."

Billie lowered her eyes. "Yes," she said. "I've known Ross since I was a girl. What did he say?"

"I told him I was ridin' for the C Heart and I was huntin' C Heart cattle. Devlin said the Rafter D and other outfits in the area have lost cattle too. He believes *rustlers* are the reason."

Billie nodded. "What about the other men?"

"They didn't give their names and I didn't ask. One was a square-jawed redhead with a broken nose. The other was a hard case with a pock-marked face and white hair down to his shoulders. I took him for a gun hand. All three men rode horses branded Rafter D."

Billie stood up. She took my plate and eating tools and put them in a dishpan on the counter. "The redhead would be Sam Bodie, cow boss of the Rafter D. As for the long-haired man, I've heard that Ross and some of the other ranchers have brought in a range detective who answers that description. I understand he's known as Maddox."

She turned back to me. "Were Ross and his men armed?"

"To the teeth. Winchesters in saddle scabbards and six-guns at their waists."

Billie looked at me with her level gaze. "A lot

of men in this country carry guns," she said. "I notice you don't."

"That's right," I said. "I don't."

Silence dropped like a curtain between us. In the stillness I heard the stove ping. Somewhere, a clock counted seconds. Was Billie waiting for me to say more?

She smiled and her voice was soft. "See you in the morning," she said. "Breakfast at four-thirty."

At the bunkhouse, Clem Guthrie was already in bed but Kip Merriday was wide awake. He sat at the table by the window, cleaning his nickel-plated gun by lamplight. As soon as I set foot inside the door, he commenced to run his mouth.

"Fanshaw, by god!" he said. "About *time* you got back! What'd you do, old timer—stop off someplace for a nap?"

"Not me," I said. "Some jobs just take longer to do *right*."

"I wouldn't know about that," he said.

"No," I said. "I don't suppose you would."

I sat on my bunk and pulled off my boots. "How long do you expect you'll be playin' with your six-shooter there, Wild Bill? I sleep better when it's dark."

"Ain't playin' with it. I'm cleanin' it. All the famous gunfighters keep their irons clean and oiled. A man never knows when he might get in a shoot-out."

"I had no idea you were a famous gunfighter, Kip. But I'll tell you what—if that *lamp* doesn't go out in the next two minutes, *you* will."

Kip told me to go to hell but he did put the lamp out, with almost a minute to spare.

BOGGED DOWN

Next morning after chuck, Billie walked over to the barn with Kip and me. The day had dawned clear and cold and the rutted mud had frozen hard as iron. In the big corral, steam rose into the morning air from the surface of the stock tank. A dozen pairs—cows and new calves— basked in the sunlight, the cows "taking the waters" at the C Heart "soup kitchen." Billie led the way to the catch pen beyond the barn where a score of horses stood watching.

"That claybank mare on the left is my horse," Billie said. "I call her Grace. She's a little contrary sometimes, but then so am I. The strawberry roan next to her is Clem's gelding, and Maggie rides that line back dun. Off to the right, by themselves, are Jack and Jill, our work team. The other horses make up the C Heart cavvy.

"I want you each to cut out three or four head for your own string. They'll be yours to use while you ride for the C Heart. They're all gentle, or at least they were before I turned them out last fall. Some may be a bit snuffy at first but they should level off after a wet saddle blanket or two. Give them a firm hand but treat them right. They'll

work for you if you let them know what you want."

Billie looked off into the distance, as if she was seeing in her mind the open country Kip and me rode the day before. "We're still missing forty cows and their calves but I don't think there's much point in continuing to hunt for them now. We'll wait for the roundup, when riders from all the brands will be combing the country. Maybe our stock will turn up then. If not . . ."

Billie cut off her sentence and turned back to Kip and me. "For the next week or so, I want you to stay close to the home place. Ride the water holes. Watch for bogged cattle and pull them out when you find them. Look for weak cows and bring them in to the 'soup kitchen.' That warm water and a little extra feed will help get them through until the new grass comes in."

"One more thing," Billie said. "Once or twice in the past we've had men on the payroll who fancied themselves bronc fighters. They abused the horses in their string and were handed their walking papers. Now I'm sure *you* men are not of that kind, but I believe in plain speaking.

"If I see 'bear sign' on any C Heart horse—spur tracks, welts, whip marks, or the like—the rider who made those marks will spool his bed, draw his time, and go off down the road. He might as well sell his saddle and take a job in a shoe store because I'll make sure every cow outfit within

two hundred miles knows about him and the reason I canned him."

Billie's face softened and she smiled. "I didn't mean to come on so war-like," she said. "It's just that I have strong *feelings* about certain things."

"You sure don't have to worry on my account," Kip said. "I'm a top hand—too good a rider to have to rough up a horse."

Billie looked at me. I smiled. "Or me, Billie," I said. "You're preachin' to the choir."

After Billie went back to the house, I took the time to look the cavvy over with an eye toward picking out my string. I was looking for good, solid mounts, steady and strong, and it didn't take me long to find three I thought would do. I chose a clear-footed dun, a blaze-faced bay with one white stocking, and a black ripper who was hell for stout. I didn't tell Kip my choices but instead offered him first pick for his own mounts. I wanted to see what kind of a judge of horse flesh he really was.

Kip sauntered among the horses, looking them over from every angle like a judge at a horse show. In the end, his choices were about what I figured they would be. He picked a flashy but fiddle-footed chestnut, a wring-tail sorrel I'd pegged for a cloud hunter, and a pretty good gray, except for it being a little light in the timber. I confess I was pleased he hadn't chosen any of

the horses I'd picked, but then I hadn't really expected him to.

I was beginning to feel a little sorry for Kip Merriday. A man who spends his life going against the grain gets more opportunities to learn humility than someone who doesn't. I figured Kip was due to graduate with honors from the School of Hard Knocks if somebody didn't kill him first.

Sometimes a man can see trouble coming a mile away. When the sky goes black on a summer's day and lightning stabs the prairie out of ragged clouds as purple as a bruise, a prudent man takes shelter where he can. If a man is careless with matches in the woods, he shouldn't be surprised if one day he has to outrun a forest fire. And when a man rides with a feisty kid whose mouth keeps writing checks his body can't cash—well, I guess that man should have known better in the first place.

There is no more thankless job on a cow outfit than riding bog. When spring comes, the cattle are weak and hungry and are ready for sunshine and new grass. Ice has gone out of the reservoirs and creeks and cows are able to get to open water again. But the water holes are oft-times boggy and the critters tend to crowd one another. Now and again one of the weaker cows gets knocked down and gets stuck in the mud. At that point it's up to a cowpuncher and a good horse to take a hand.

If the critter is stuck bad enough it may take two men to free it; one who takes hold of its horns and one who gets a tail hold. Then, once the cow is on its feet, the man in front runs for his horse and then the tail holder does. With luck, and if their horses are far enough away, the riders escape with only muddy feet and clothes.

So it was later in the week that Kip and me came across a stuck cow at a water hole two miles north of the ranch. I was riding a big black horse Billie called Old Ebenezer, and Kip was astraddle of the fiddle-footed chestnut he'd picked for his string. Billie allowed her riders to use the bath house and Kip was clean and pink from his evening ablutions. I have to admit he was the very picture of the dashing range rider, in a checkered shirt, sleeve garters, and a silk kerchief loose-knotted about his throat. A rawhide quirt hung by a thong from his right wrist. Beneath his wide-brimmed hat, his hair was slicked back and pomaded. I suppose he would have been clean-shaven too if he'd had any whiskers. He sported high-topped boots, spurs of Mexican design, and of course his pearl-handled pistol. Young Kip Merriday was pretty as a sunrise.

The cow was a brockle-faced Durham, and she was not a happy bovine. The cow lay mired to her belly in a boggy patch marked by the tracks of stronger, more fortunate cattle. She had stopped struggling some time before, but that didn't mean

she accepted her fate. She rolled her eyes and gave us a mournful bellow that was both a complaint and a cry for help. The old girl was in tough shape and a bad mood.

I took down my rope and built a loop. Kip looked like he'd rather be anywhere else but next to a mud hole full of cow. He said nothing, but his lower lip stuck out far enough to make a perch for a dickie bird.

I grinned at Kip. "Well," I said. "She's no damsel but she sure is in distress. What will you take, heads or tails?"

"Damn, Fanshaw," he grumbled. "Can't we just pretend we didn't *see* this one?"

"No, I don't believe we can," I said. I stepped down off Ebenezer and waded out into the muck. "I'll take her head. Get on in here and tail her up."

Kip made a decision. "Hell no," he said. "I *won't,* by god."

"You might want to think about that. You're drawin' pay as a cow hand. If you won't do the work, you won't keep the job."

"I didn't hire on to waller in no damn mud hole. I'm a top hand and a *horse* man. Only work *I'll* do is the kind I can do from a horse's back."

I was fresh out of patience. "I'm *tired* of your bull, Kip. Far as I can see, you're not much of a hand at all, and you sure as hell aren't a 'top' hand."

"Yeah? We'll just *see* about that," he said.

"Come up out of that mud hole, you sonofabitch! I'm gonna clean your clock!"

Kip jerked the chestnut's head around, swinging his right leg free as he went to step down. His right-hand spur hooked the gelding in its flank and caused the animal to jump. Half off, half on, Kip clutched the saddle horn and reins, trying to keep from being thrown. The horse then panicked, spinning to its off side as Kip hung on with a death grip.

Confused and frightened, the chestnut blew up and fell to bucking. Kip held on for the first jump or two before being thrown free. He struck the ground hard but got quickly to his feet, still clenching the reins in his left hand. The frightened chestnut tried to back away, and then reared up on its hind legs as Kip lashed out at its neck and head with his rawhide quirt. His face distorted by rage, Kip seemed almost to have forgotten I was even there.

"*Goddammit!*" Kip shouted. "I'll learn *you* to spook at shadows!"

And he slashed at the chestnut again.

I was on him by then, mud and all. When Kip drew back his arm to strike the horse again, I grabbed the quirt and jerked. The strap that held the quirt to Kip's wrist pulled him away from the chestnut and onto the ground. I jerked again and the strap broke.

Reversing the quirt, I waited as Kip scrambled

to his feet. Then I sidestepped and brought the quirt down hard across his backside. He cried out in pain and surprise, and I lashed him again—once, twice, and a third time—as he tried to block my blows with his arms.

"*Smarts,* don't it?" I asked. "*Damn* a man who'd mistreat a horse!"

Kip lowered his head and came at me in a rush. I sidestepped his charge and caught him full in face with an uppercut that met him halfway. Kip went down like a puppet with its strings cut.

I bent over him and pulled his pearl-handled pistol from the leather. Stunned, he looked up at me and I saw his eyes regain their focus. I held out the gun so he could see it. "This whole ruckus started because you didn't want to get muddy," I said. "Well, you're goin' to *have* to if you ever want to see your six-shooter again." And I threw the gun as far out into the bog as I could.

I didn't wait to see what Kip would do. Instead, I swung up on Old Ebenezer and dabbed a loop around the bogged cow's head. Riding the big gelding off into the muck ahead of the cow, I took my dallies and headed for dry ground. The cow's neck stretched about as far as it could without leaving her body, and then she broke free of the mire and slid up onto the grassy bank. Before she could get up and make a run at me, I dismounted, slipped my loop off her horns, and swung back into the saddle.

Kip had waded out into the mire and was searching for his six-gun. I nearly felt sorry for him until I recalled the way he'd used his quirt on the chestnut. I rode Ebenezer over to where the gelding stood and picked up its reins.

"I'm takin' your horse back to the ranch," I said. "The walk will give you a chance to cool down and repent of your wicked ways."

Turning Ebenezer away, I left Kip a parting word, "If you want to take this further, I won't be hard to find."

Billie was at the barn when I got back to the ranch. She and Clem were doctoring a sick calf, but they both stopped what they were doing when they saw me ride in leading Kip's chestnut. Billie watched as I opened the corral gate and took both horses inside. Then she dried her hands on a towel and walked over to me.

"Calf with the scours," she said. "Don't know if we've saved him or not."

I was muddy from the water hole, and so was the big gelding I rode. Billie looked us over. "Find a critter bogged down?" she asked.

I nodded. "That brockle-faced dry cow," I said. "Old Ebenezer popped her out of the mud like a cork from a bottle."

Billie's eyes went to the chestnut. The welts from Kip's quirt were plain on the animal's head and shoulders. Billie reached out and touched the gelding's neck. When she looked back at me her

wide brown eyes were as hard as agate. "What happened?" she asked. "Where's Kip?"

"You might say Kip and me had a difference of opinion. As for where he is, I expect he'll be along directly."

"Are those his quirt marks?"

"They're not mine."

"I want it all, Merlin. What happened?"

"We had words. The chestnut spooked and put Kip on the ground. He took his mad out on the horse."

"And then?"

"I took his quirt away and showed him how it felt to be on the receiving end."

"After which you set him afoot?"

"I figured the chestnut had enough of Kip Merriday for one day."

Billie nodded. "Yes," she said. "I'm sure it has."

"There's a jar of salve and some clean cloths in the tack room," Billie said. "You might want to take care of that horse's cuts and welts."

"Yes," I said. "I sure might."

Billie looked into my eyes and smiled a quick, distracted smile. Some of the hardness had left her eyes but anger remained, and sadness. She turned quickly away, walking back to Clem and the calf.

I led the chestnut into the barn, stripped it of its saddle and bridle, and placed it in a stall. I found the cloths and salve Billie had mentioned and

doctored the gelding's wounds. I felt my own anger rise in my throat. Kip's quirt had drawn blood in several places, and one cut had barely missed the horse's eye.

When I left the barn, I found Clem Guthrie waiting for me. "Couldn't help but overhear what you told Billie," he said. "I wish I could have seen you take a quirt to that pup. He's had it comin' for awhile."

I shrugged. "Maybe. The kid doesn't really bother me all that much. He talks big because he feels small. Most of the time I can just let his chin music roll off like water off a duck. But I did lose my head some when he commenced to abuse his horse."

Clem frowned. Then he cleared his throat and said, "Just because he's a blowhard don't mean he ain't dangerous. I'd watch my back if I was you."

"It's hard for a man to watch his back when his eyes are in his front," I said. "But I'll do my best."

I was waiting at the corral when Kip Merriday came sore-footing back to the ranch. He was red-faced and mud-covered, and his once proud swagger had become a painful limp. He had walked through two miles of cactus and rocks in his high-heeled boots, and from the look of him it had not been a pleasant experience. I'll never know how long it took him to find and recover his

fancy revolver, but find it he had. The pistol's pearl handles showed plain atop the open holster at his waist.

I stepped away from the corral as he approached and met him in the road. Kip stopped, staring at me through slitted eyes. His hand hovered above the pistol's grips. "I ain't scared of you," he said.

"If you say so," I replied.

Kip looked down at the ground. "I . . . I'm sorry about whippin' on my horse thataway," he said. "I never meant to."

"A little temper in a man is a good thing," I said. "Long as it doesn't run him."

I suppose we might have gone on that way all afternoon, talking in short bursts and acting like two ragamuffins in a schoolyard, but right then Billie came out of the main house and strode toward us across the barn lot.

Stepping between us, Billie handed Kip a gold eagle and a half eagle in coin. "There's two weeks pay due you," she said. "Roll your bed and hitch up the team. Clem will drive you to town."

"I don't know what Fanshaw told you—"

"The welts and cuts on the chestnut speak for themselves," Billie said. "I believe I gave you fair warning."

Kip nodded. "You can tie a can to my tail if you want to," he said, "but I'll be ridin' for another outfit before the week is out. I'm a top hand."

Then he gave me a hard look and swaggered

away toward the horse pasture. Kip Merriday may have been a slow learner, but he did have a certain style.

It was late afternoon when I heard the wagon coming up the lane. I walked out onto the bunkhouse porch, watching as Clem reined the team to a stop at the main house. He stepped down and picked up a good-sized box from the back, which he then carried into the house. *Not a bad trade,* I thought; *Kip Merriday for a box of groceries.*

I walked over to the barn lot and waited. Minutes later, Clem drove up and parked the rig. "Figured I'd help you unhitch," I said.

"Good of you," Clem said. "Maggie says supper's in thirty minutes."

A man didn't need to be much of a detective to know Clem had visited a saloon before coming home. His face was flushed, and he was in a mellow mood.

As though he read my mind, Clem said, "Stopped in at the Mint Saloon for a drink or two," he said, "after I got shut of what's his name. Seemed like a reason to celebrate."

I grinned. "When a man wants a drink, *anything's* a reason to celebrate."

"I suppose," Clem said. "*Another* reason is I need to live up to my reputation. Billie told you I'm a good judge of whiskey and men."

I laughed. "She also said you're about half worthless these days, but I don't see you celebratin' that."

Clem's smile widened. "Well," he said, "even Billie can't be right about *everything*."

We walked together back to the bunkhouse. "What's the latest news in Fairfax?" I asked.

Clem's expression turned serious. "Hard talk about rustlers," he said. "Accordin' to the bar crowd, everybody who doesn't ride for one of the *big* outfits is probably a cow thief."

"Bar talk comes cheap," I said.

"It's more than talk. The Mint was full of Texas *pistoleros*. They say Ross Devlin and some of the other big operators brought in a trainload of them."

"Gun hands?"

"Nothin' but. They're *callin'* themselves *regulators*—which is just a fancy name for hired killers, if you ask me. That long-haired 'range detective' you ran into—Maddox—is supposed to head up the bunch, on orders from the big ranchers."

"You believe that?" I asked.

"I don't know enough *not* to," said Clem.

Seven

COMING AND GOING

During the next few weeks Clem Guthrie and me were pretty much the entire crew of the C Heart. I rode bog, moved the weak stock down to the home ranch, and worked my string of horses. Clem and me spent two days cleaning out waterholes with the work team and a slip, and mended some of the old pasture fences.

Billie's nearest neighbor, a homesteader named Irv Baker, lived ten miles west of the C Heart on Sage Creek. Irv was poor in property but rich in progeny, scratching out a living on a farm that was mostly rock and sagebrush while raising three sons and two daughters.

Billie hired Irv's sixteen-year-old twins, Jake and Alex, to irrigate her hay meadows and help out with the ranch work. Unlike the recently departed Kip Merriday, the Baker boys were early risers whose hard work belied the saying, "If you have two kids working for you and you want to get more done, fire one of them."

We all liked the Baker boys, but they seemed to occupy a special place in Maggie's heart. Maggie delighted in coming up with special desserts and such, and the twins showed their appreciation by

wolfing them down. With all the mouths their pa had to feed at home, I reckon Maggie's kitchen must have seemed to the boys like the Horn of Plenty.

Somewhere around the middle of May, Maggie asked me to spade up a patch of ground next to the front porch for a vegetable garden. I was well begun on the job one morning when I saw an open buggy coming up the lane. Drawn by a high-stepping black gelding, the buggy was black as well, gleaming in the sunlight as it crossed the bridge and turned onto the barn lot.

The driver, a well-dressed man in a dark suit and silver belly Stetson, seemed familiar to me. I narrowed my eyes, trying to remember where and when I'd seen him. Then, as he drew rein in front of the house, I recognized him. He was Ross Devlin, owner of the Rafter D and the man I'd run into the day I was out hunting Billie's cows.

Devlin looked at the house and smiled. Then he looped the reins around the whip socket and stepped down. He didn't look my way, and somehow I knew he hadn't come to see me. Next thing I knew, Billie walked out of the house and met him at the gate.

"Good morning, Ross," she said. "A little off your range, aren't you?"

He doffed his hat and smiled. I don't believe I ever saw such white teeth on a man.

"Would you believe me if I said I just happened to be out this way and thought I'd pay you a friendly visit?"

Billie laughed. "Probably not," she said, "but I might pretend to, for courtesy's sake."

She took his arm. "Come on inside," she said. "It's a warm morning. We'll have coffee on the porch."

On the porch! Beside the porch is where I was working! If I stayed where I was I'd hear every word they said!

On the other hand, I couldn't very well just get up and leave. I was right in the middle of planting a row of carrots for Maggie. Besides, it was too late. I suppose I could have said, "Scuse me, folks, I'm a-workin' here next to the porch," but that might embarrass Billie. Or Ross might think I was spying on him. I decided to keep mum and tend to my business, even if it meant I might overhear their conversation. Which, of course, I did.

I heard footfall, chairs sliding on the hardwood floor of the screen porch. Then the clink of china cups on saucers. Ross said, "How do you do it, Billie? You seem to grow more beautiful with time. You're a vision for this old man's eyes."

Billie's voice: "You're not an old man, Ross. But you might consider having your eyes checked. The truth is I grow more weathered and worn every day."

"This place is too much for you. Sell me the C Heart and let me take care of you."

"We've covered this ground before, Ross. The C Heart is not for sale, and neither am I."

"I did not mean it that way," Ross said. "You know how I feel about you."

"Yes," Billie said. "I think I do. I won't embarrass you by asking if 'taking care of me' includes a ring."

There was silence for a moment. Then Ross said, "I met a young cowboy this week, up on the Mizpah. Said his name was Merlin Fanshaw and that he's riding for the C Heart. I didn't know you were hiring."

"I needed help," Billie said. "When Merlin came along, there was only Clem and me to work the place. Merlin has more than made a hand since he showed up."

"I understand you're missing some stock."

"Yes. Forty pairs, give or take."

"Most of the cow men I know are short on their head counts, including me. I believe rustlers are working the Big Open."

"I hear you've brought in a stock detective and some . . . *regulators.*"

"As Granville Stuart did, back in '84. Jim Fergus summed it up that year. 'We must gather up what stock we have left and leave the country,' he said, 'or gather up these desperados and put them where they will kill and steal no more; there

is no alternative, and we choose the latter. It is now simply a state of war.' "

"Vigilantes make mistakes," Billie said.

"So do peace officers and the courts. We will do what we have to."

"What does all this have to do with me?"

"It's just that we all have to be careful about hiring strangers."

"Like Merlin? Merlin has my full confidence."

"A friendly warning, Billie. That's all I came to give you."

I heard the chair legs scrape the floor. "Thank you for your concern, Ross. Now I have a warning for *you*. Be careful about taking the law into your own hands. You can't unhang a man."

Again, I heard the scraping of chair legs. "Thank you for the coffee, Billie," Ross said. "You not only grow more beautiful with time, but more spirited. An exciting combination."

A moment later, the screen door banged. Ross Devlin strode the plank walkway to his horse and buggy, took the reins, and drove away back down the lane. His face was set like stone, and he didn't wave back at Billie.

Looking down at the row I'd just planted, I found I'd put onion seed in the same holes where I'd planted carrots.

My respect for Billie Hart grew greater each day. She was soft-spoken, but firm on matters of

principle. Like all good bosses, Billie never asked the people who worked for her to do anything she wouldn't do herself. She seldom gave orders as such, but instead *asked* her workers to perform their tasks. "Merlin," she would say, "when you have time, would you move those cows down to the lower pasture?" Or, "That black gelding has sand cracks in his rear hooves. Would you mind trimming his feet and putting new shoes on him?"

Billie was a fine horsewoman, and a better roper than I was myself. She sat a horse with her back straight and her shoulders level, and a man could tell she was the boss of the outfit just by looking at her. At the same time, Billie was a sure-enough woman, and a mighty handsome one. I guess I shouldn't have thought about her in that way, but I did sometimes. What's more, there were times I wished she'd think about *me* in that way, too.

She was outgoing and cheerful, but sometimes when she thought no one was watching, she would pull back into some quiet place of her own and shut the world outside. Then her smile would fade and a frown would take its place. She would seem unmindful of people around her. Her face would change and she would appear as she did the day I met her, when she and Clem were trying to help the heifer. Her expression on that day had been one of worry and concern. When these moods came upon her, I wondered what their

cause might be. More than that, I longed to be the one who brought her smile back.

I mentioned Billie's moods to Clem one night at the bunkhouse, and he just shook his head. "Billie has her troubles," is all he would say.

It occurred to me that at least one of Billie's troubles might be the forty missing C Heart pairs. Neither Kip nor I had found a trace of them, and Billie seemed resigned to wait for the roundup and hope they'd turn up. Maybe they would. Riders from all the ranches would comb the Big Open then and sort out the branded and unbranded stock they found.

On the other hand, if the rumors of rustlers were true, Billie's cattle might well be held by thieves in some hidden badlands canyon to be herded out of the area by night.

It was a slack time. The Baker twins and Clem could handle what little work there was to do around the place. We wouldn't be branding at the C Heart for a week or so. It would, I thought, be a good time for a lone rider to coyote the rims and have himself a look-see.

I made my pitch to Billie. "We're pretty well caught up around here for the time being," I said. "I'd like to take another try at finding your missing cattle."

I saw hope rise in her eyes. "You and Kip didn't find anything when you looked before."

"The Big Open is well named," I said. "We

probably didn't cover five percent of that country. I'd like to take a pack horse, maybe stay out a week or so and see what I can find."

Billie considered my words. For a long moment she was silent. Then she asked, "Will you carry a gun?"

I shook my head. "No," I said. "I won't pack a six-gun. I'm huntin' cows, not trouble."

She smiled. "Most people who *find* trouble were hunting something else at the time."

Billie raised her eyes to the distant hills, seeming to weigh and balance my offer. At length, she turned back to me and met my eyes. "All right," she said, "but only if you take a rifle.

"Maybe, if trouble sees you've got a Winchester it will leave you alone. What do you say?"

I laughed. "I don't think that's how it works," I said. "But all right, Billie. It's a deal."

After breakfast the next day, I ran in the clear-footed dun and the blaze-faced bay and made ready to ride the Big Open. The Baker twins sauntered into the barn as I was putting my camp outfit together. One of them (I'm not sure which; I still couldn't tell the boys apart) helped me balance my packs and throw a one-man diamond hitch on the dun.

"Miss Billie says you're ridin' out for a few days," said one of the twins.

"That's right," I replied.

"You ain't by any chance goin' past our home place, are you? It ain't but seven mile from here, down on Sage Creek."

"I can," I said. "What do you need?"

The twin handed me an envelope. He said, "Miss Billie paid us for the week. My brother and me was wonderin' if you'd maybe take our wages to our folks. They could sure use some cash money."

I took the envelope. "You boys are good workers," I said. "I'll tell your folks that."

Two matching smiles were my reward. I took the dun's lead rope, swung up onto the bay, and rode out into the morning.

I found the Baker homestead a half hour later, above the muddy waters of Sage Creek. Cut into the flank of a low, grassy hill and choked by weeds, the family's first home had been a bare-bones dugout, low and mean. Now abandoned, its sod roof tumbled in and its front wall collapsed, it seemed to serve notice that farming the Big Open was a chancy proposition at best.

But the Bakers hadn't quit. A sod-roofed house and a rough barn, built of cottonwood logs, stood up the slope from the creek. Near the house, a rail-thin woman and a girl tended a small garden. The woman straightened, shading her eyes to watch me.

At the barn, a thick-bodied man I took to be Irv Baker was also watching me. He turned away,

disappearing into the shadows. When he came out again, he held a short-barreled rifle at the ready.

I raised my right hand as I rode toward him and smiled. He didn't smile back, and he didn't ease his grip on the rifle. Looking beyond him at the corral fence, I saw the reason why. The fresh hide of a Durham steer was draped over the top rail. The brand was clear: Rafter D.

I drew rein and tried to look harmless. "Mornin'," I said. "Are you Irv Baker?"

"Who wants to know?" he asked.

"Merlin Fanshaw," I said. "I ride for the C Heart. Your boys asked me to stop by."

Some of the suspicion left his face, but he still held the rifle.

"Jake and Alex? You know my boys?"

"Sure do," I said. "I don't always know which one is which, but I know them. They're good boys and hard workers."

Irv Baker looked relieved. He stared at the rifle, passing it from hand to hand as if he didn't quite know what to do with it. Finally, he propped it against the barn and grinned.

"Sorry," he said. "I never meant to come on so hostile. Guess I'm gettin' nervous in my old age."

I said nothing, but my eyes went again to the green cowhide.

Baker caught my glance. "You're lookin' at the hide," he said. "Ross Devlin allows us to butcher a steer now and again."

"A lot of the big outfits have that policy," I said, "or used to. But the times are changin'."

Baker frowned. "Yeah," he said. "I heard somethin' about that. Hired guns ridin' for the big ranchers. 'Regulators,' they call themselves."

I took the envelope from the inside pocket of my vest. "Jake and Alex sent you this," I said. "It's their first week's wages from the C Heart."

Baker's hand trembled as he took the envelope from me. He cleared his throat. "My children are my shinin' pride. A man wishes he could do better for his family."

"I haven't met your whole family," I said, "but from what I've seen of Jake and Alex, I'd say you're doin' all right."

Baker just nodded, as if he didn't trust his voice. Then, after a moment, he said, "I've plumb forgot my manners," he said. "Why don't you get down and come meet the rest of my family. That's my wife Martha in the garden with Sally, my youngest daughter. My oldest girl, Ruthie, is in the house ridin' herd on baby Luke."

"Much obliged," I said, "but I've got range to cover. Another time."

Baker reached up and we shook hands. "Another time, then," he said. "You're more than welcome."

I turned my horses away from Irv Baker's hard rock farm. Far to the west, big-bellied storm clouds darkened the sky and rain hung from their

lower edge like cobwebs. Lightning stabbed the plains and thunder rolled. I don't necessarily believe in omens, but for just a moment there I was afraid for Irv Baker and his family.

For the rest of that first day I rode the ridges between Powder River and Mizpah Creek, covering some of the same country I had before. The wind picked up and commenced to bluster and bully the land. Twice, I reached back to untie the strings that held my slicker, but each time the clouds broke and the storm passed over.

Not that it *couldn't* have rained and rained a-plenty. I have been caught out in cloudbursts and gully washers more than once, and I never take a prairie squall for granted. At the same time, I know the scariest thunderstorm is oft-times long on bluster and short on rain. I left my 'fish' tied behind my cantle and called the tempest's bluff.

I saw scattered bunches of cattle that day, some cow-calf pairs and a few steers, but nothing that wore Billie's brand. Most of the livestock I saw were either marked Rafter D or other brands I was not familiar with.

I made camp that evening on a hill overlooking Powder River. At first I thought I'd bed down along the riverbank, but the durned skeeters were so thick I changed my mind. I knew it was possible I might run into a snake or two up on that rocky hillside, but I decided to take my chances.

I'd almost rather be snake-bit than be set upon by clouds of whining blood-suckers.

Morning dawned cold and clear. My hobbled ponies cropped new grass along the slope while I ate a modest breakfast and shivered myself warm. As the sun's first rays painted the hilltops I watched the shadows fade and welcomed the day. Then I packed up the dun, saddled the blaze-faced bay, and rode out to look for Billie's cattle.

Eight
A HITCH IN TIME

For most of that forenoon I rode the ridges and badlands beyond Mizpah Creek, looking for a box canyon or hidden hollow that might hold stolen cattle. If rustlers were operating on the range, they'd likely be putting a herd together in just such a place. I rode up timbered coulees and through thickets of brush and scrub cedar in my search, but I found nothing. Except for a few scattered bunches of cattle far out on the plain and now and then an antelope or two, the land seemed silent and empty of life.

It must have been sometime around ten o'clock when I caught the smell of smoke. I was riding up a rocky hill that looked down on a stream and a grove of good-sized cottonwoods. *Where there's smoke there's humans,* I thought.

When I reached the crest of the ridge, I came upon a scene that made the hairs on the back of my neck stand up. At the foot of the hill, a rider in a black hat and checkered shirt had a steer down and hog-tied. His saddlehorse stood some distance away and gray smoke rose from a cow chip fire. The man bent over the steer, his right hand gripping crossed willow sticks and a cinch

106

ring. I had stumbled onto a long rope artist at work and no mistake.

I slid the Winchester from its sleeve and stepped off the bay. My hands trembled as I jacked a shell into the chamber. I took a deep breath to steady myself and started down the slope.

The rustler raised his head and froze, but he wasn't looking at me. Instead, his eyes were fixed on something off to his right. I followed his stare but saw nothing. When I looked back, I saw he had dropped the cinch ring and was striding toward his horse at a near lope. I made my way on down the hill, my boot heels digging deep, but the man was already in the saddle and whipping both ways as he left the country.

I drew up at the bottom of the hill. The steer wore a Rafter D brand. The animal lay on its side, struggling against the tie-rope that bound its legs. It rolled its eyes and bawled. And six men rode into the clearing on lathered horses.

Ross Devlin was in the lead. He reined his horse to a sliding stop, his arm raised in signal to the men behind him. I recognized the man called Maddox and the square-jawed redhead Billie said was Sam Bodie. All six were armed with six-guns and carbines, and they all seemed to be pointing them at me.

"Drop it!" Devlin said.

Raising my left hand, I bent my knees and laid the Winchester on the ground. I looked up at Ross

Devlin and showed him both hands, held high and empty. Dust billowed up from the horses' hooves. Bodie stepped down and picked up the rifle. The other three riders circled around behind me.

"Caught you red-handed, you sonofabitch," said Bodie.

I knew how the layout must look to them. Steer tied and on the ground. Twisted willows holding a hot cinch ring. Smoking cow chip fire.

Hadn't they seen the rider in the checkered shirt?

"Not me," I said. "The rope and ring man quit the country when he heard you comin'."

"You lyin' sack o' shit," Bodie said. "Only rope and ring man *I* see is *you*."

I looked at Devlin again. He met my eyes, his face hard as an axe blade. I saw him nod at Bodie in some signal of their own, and then he turned his horse and rode away at a trot.

Still holding my Winchester, Bodie stepped up close to me and took a wide stance. "I can't abide a goddamn cow thief," he said.

He swung the butt of the carbine up and caught me beneath the jaw. Bright light flared behind my eyes. I staggered, stunned by the blow, and nearly went down. Pain exploded inside my head. Then I heard a rope whistle behind me and a noose closed about my neck.

"Take him down to them cottonwoods," Bodie said. "We'll *hang* the bastard!"

I felt the rope tighten. I managed to get my fingers inside the noose, but the roper behind me took a wrap around his saddle horn and spurred his horse toward the tree line. I fell, choking, and was dragged through the dirt on my way to the trees. Once there, the rider pulled up and tossed the free end of the rope over a limb.

It all happened so fast I didn't even have time to be scared. But now I saw my own death coming and there was nothing I could do about it. I was near to blacking out, the rope had cut off my wind, and I couldn't even beg for my life. I saw Bodie's face, pitiless and grim. The man called Maddox grinned a wolfish grin, his eyes wild. And I was jerked off the ground and into the air.

Then a gunshot rang out. Bark flew from the cottonwood's trunk. I felt the rope go slack. My feet touched the ground, and I sprawled headlong.

The eyes of every rider were focused on a spot back near where the steer lay. I jerked the loop open and thrust the rope over my head. Struggling to get to my feet, I tried to see what the riders saw. And then I did.

Hitch Holbrook!

The line rider for the Claymore Cattle Company sat his blue roan with an easy grace. His left hand gripped the horse's reins and the rifle's forestock, and his right hand kept the Winchester trained on the "regulators."

"Is this necktie party *private*," he drawled, "or can *anyone* come?"

Caught off guard, the riders gave Holbrook their full attention. Maddox inched his hand toward the holstered revolver at his hip. Sam Bodie, his feet spread wide in the loose dirt, was the first to find his voice. "Who the hell are *you?*" he asked.

"Why, I'm a man with a *rifle,*" Holbrook replied. "Who the hell are *you?*"

Tense as a coiled snake, Maddox moved his hand closer to the grips of his gun.

"I'm Sam Bodie, cow boss of the Rafter D," Bodie said. "We were just fixin' to hang us a rustler."

Holbrook shifted the Winchester to Maddox. "Touch that hog leg, long hair, and *you* die *first.*"

Maddox jerked his hand away from his gun as if it was hot.

Holbrook's eyes moved to the other riders. "That goes for you boys, too. Don't make any sudden moves, and keep your hands clear of your irons."

Bodie's face was flushed. "Damn it!" he said. "Who *are* you?" Pointing at me, he asked, "Are you this man's partner? That's a Rafter D steer up yonder . . . we caught this thief dead to rights!"

"Wrong," Holbrook said. "The *real* thief is a man in a black hat and checkered shirt. I was watchin' through my long glass from that sand-

rock butte back yonder. He lit out for the tall and uncut when he heard you boys comin'."

I was getting my wind back, but my neck felt like it was on fire. The pain in my jaw where Bodie butt-stroked me with my carbine throbbed like a war drum.

Bodie turned to me. "Then . . . who are you?" he asked.

It hurt my throat, but I needed to talk. "Merlin Fanshaw," I croaked. "Like I told you *last* week—I ride for the C Heart."

Flustered but trying to cover it, Bodie turned again to Holbrook. "You still haven't said who *you* are," he said.

"That's right," Holbrook said.

Bodie handed my Winchester back. It was as near to an apology as I was likely to have.

He gave Hitch a hard look. Then he turned back to his horse and swung into the saddle.

"We've wasted enough time," he said to the other men. "Somebody cut that steer loose, and we'll dust the hell out of here."

One of the riders cut the rope that bound the steer, swung back in the saddle and rode out with the others. Bodie held his head high as he led the riders away, and he didn't look at Hitch and me again. Maddox did, though. He slowed his horse as he passed us, his cold gray eyes fixed on each of us as if he was committing our features to memory.

111

When the riders had gone, Hitch slid his carbine into its scabbard. "You all right?" he asked.

I didn't much feel like talking, so I just grinned and raised my eyebrows. My jaw was hurting in earnest by then, and my neck reminded me it wasn't used to such treatment. After a minute I rasped, "How . . . How did . . ."

"Huntin' Claymore cows," Hitch said. "Saw y'all when you topped out on the ridge and stepped off your hoss. I looked to see what *you* saw, and spotted the steer and the man in the checkered shirt. When them boys jumped you, it occurred to me you might need a little help."

"I'm obliged," I croaked.

Hitch shrugged. "Hell," he said. "It's nothin' personal. I just can't abide a damn lynch mob."

Then he turned his roan and rode away toward the river.

For awhile I just stood there, thinking how close I'd come to dying. I breathed in the cool, clean air and tasted its sweetness. Blue mountains slept in sunlight at the edge of the world. Prairie grasses and sagebrush stood out in sharp relief. I seemed to see everything as if for the first time. I was glad to be alive, grateful even for the pain where the rope had burned my neck. Only the living feel pain, I thought. Catching my rifle in the crook of my arm, I hiked up the hill to where I'd left my horses.

• • •

By the time I got back to the C Heart, my jaw had swole up near twice its normal size. My tongue felt big as a cow's, and pain stabbed through me with every step of the blaze-faced bay. I drew rein at the barn and eased down to the ground.

Clem stepped out of the barn and into sunlight. He stood in the doorway, leaning on a manure fork. "You're back early," he said. "Did you find . . ."

Clem shaded his eyes against the brightness and took a closer look. I must have been a sight, for he dropped the fork and shambled toward me across the corral. "Lordamighty!" he said. "What happened to you?"

"Had a run-in with Devlin's regulators. They were on the prod."

He opened the gate and stepped up close, staring at my face. "I declare!" he said. "You look like a chipmunk eatin' a persimmon! Are you all right, son?"

"I've been better," I allowed. "Let me take care o' these ponies and I'll tell you about it."

Well, nothing would do but that Clem would give me a hand. I never asked him to, but by the time I'd stripped the saddle and bridle from the bay he'd unpacked the dun and put him in a stall. When he came out again, he had a pint of whiskey in his hand. He drew the cork and handed me the bottle.

I shook my head and winced. "Much obliged,"

I said, "but I'm not much of a whiskey drinker."

"This ain't whiskey," Clem said. "It's a combination painkiller and conversation fluid. Good for what ails you."

I took a drink and handed the bottle back. "You lied, but I forgive you," I said. "I may become a whiskey drinker yet."

I hunkered down in the shade and took my hat off. My sweated brow felt cool in its absence. Clem corked the bottle and squatted beside me.

"Well?" he said. "I'm all ears."

I grinned and caught my breath. Pain stabbed like lightning through my swollen jaw, and it was a moment or two before I could answer him.

Clem's eyes were the color of faded denim. He fixed his gaze on me, waiting for my response.

"All *ears,* are you?" I said. "Yeah, I've *noticed* that about you, Clem. All right. . . ." With my voice strained from the hemp necktie and my jaw throbbing with every word, I gave account of my morning with Devlin and his regulators. I told the story simple and direct, neither wasting words nor allowing for questions, and when I'd told it all I stopped. Leaning back against the barn wall, I shut my eyes and rested my voice box.

At first Clem was speechless, which I have to tell you was not his usual condition. The old man's face turned beet red and he seemed to stare off into space at nothing. I figured he was going

over the events I'd described in his mind's eye. When at last he broke the silence, his voice was tight as a drumhead.

"Damn that highfalutin' Ross Devlin!" he said. "Chicken-hearted sum'bitch set his hired killers on you and then rode off so he couldn't be blamed for what happened!

"I've knowed Ross since he was a kid. Knowed his daddy, Horace, before him. Horace spoiled Ross—gave him too much money and not enough character. I never *did* cotton to the boy."

"Can't say I blame him all that much," I whispered. "The layout sure made me look guilty—hog-tied steer, cow chip fire, and a hot runnin' iron."

Clem scowled. "They could have let you tell your story," he said.

He was silent for a moment. Then he said, "Lucky for you that line rider showed up. What did you say his name is?"

"Hitch Holbrook. I stayed at his camp when I was ridin' the grub line. It was the day before I met you and Billie."

"What about the *real* thief—the ranny in the checkered shirt? Ever see him before?"

"Maybe," I said. "I'm not sure."

Clem's glance was sharp. "Well, who do you think he *might* be?"

"I wouldn't want to say."

"Damn, Merlin! You came within a whisker of

stretchin' hemp on account of him! This ain't no time to be close-mouthed!"

I stood up. "Fact is I *did* stretch hemp, before Holbrook crashed the party! It's the second time in my life I've been strung up, and I can't say I cared for it much either time."

I had already talked more than I intended to, but I had to say the rest. "And because I *don't* know for sure who mister checkered shirt is, it's the *perfect* time to be close-mouthed. Those boys nearly lynched *one* innocent man today; I'll not accuse another unless I know for certain!"

Clem clamped his mouth tight shut and looked down at the ground. When he raised his head there was remorse in his eyes. "By god, you're right," he said. "Sorry, Merlin. I reckon I got carried away some. You know what curiosity done to the cat."

I put a hand on his shoulder. "It's all right, Clem," I said. "Now if it's all the same to you, I'm goin' to quit talkin' for awhile. Maybe amble on over to the bunkhouse and take me a lie-down."

"You bet," said Clem. "You do that, son."

Ambling on over to the bunkhouse was easier said than done. My jaw throbbed, my throat felt like I'd swallowed hot coals, and my personal carcass had more aches and pains than an old soldier's home. I made it to the bunkhouse all right, but for the last fifty yards I was afraid I

might have to drop down on all fours and crawl. I clumb up onto the raised porch and limped through the doorway. For a mercy the place was empty. When I got to my bunk, I flopped down on it and passed out like a January bear.

I don't know how long I slept, but I came awake with the notion somebody had entered the bunkhouse and was watching me sleep. I swung my legs over the side of the bed, and the pain in my jaw woke up too. Billie Hart, my boss, was watching me from the doorway, her face somber.

"Billie?" I said.

"Clem told me what happened. Are you all right?"

My voice was a hoarse whisper. "Clem shouldn't have bothered you."

Billie approached my bunk, her eyes wide and filled with concern. "He figured it was my business," she said. "So do I."

I tried to make light of the whole thing. "A misunderstandin' mostly. When those Rafter D boys saw me standin' next to their hog-tied steer, they sort of jumped to conclusions."

"Ross Devlin was with them?"

"At first. Then he rode on and left me with Sam Bodie and the others."

Billie reached out and touched my swollen face. Both her touch and her voice were gentle. "Go over to the bath house," she said. "Soak awhile in

that hot water and steam. Then come on up to the house for supper."

Her touch and her nearness flustered me some. "Yes'm," I said. "But the way my jaw feels, I don't know as I'll be able to eat much."

Her smile was as tender as her touch. "I'll have Maggie cook up some of her special broken jaw soup," she said.

I smiled back, not caring that it hurt. "Sounds good," I said. "A heap better than *graveyard* stew anyway."

A Bath and a Wagon Ride

The bath house stood four square and solid on a green patch of grass above the creek. Cattails grew in the marshy ground below the building, and steam from the well head drifted up into the morning's blue sky. Heavy planks, chalk white from minerals in the heated water, formed the building, and the smell of sulfur perfumed the air. I opened the door and peered inside.

A big wooden tub took up most of the space. At its head, a rusty valve dripped hot water, and green moss grew along the tub's sides and bottom. I closed the door behind me and waited for my eyes to grow accustomed to the gloom. A boot-jack on the floor helped me to shuck my boots and a nail on the wall provided a place to hang my duds and towel. Slipping out of my clothes, I stepped into the tub and opened the valve.

Water thundered in with a rush and hammered me into submission. I caught my breath and hung on for dear life. Hot water filled the tub and I feared at first I would be scalded like a pullet in a stew pot. I recalled hearing somewhere about the bullfrog who sat in a kettle of water that was

slowly heated until it boiled him, and all the time mister frog didn't realize he was in trouble. I had some concern I might suffer a similar fate, but the tub filled, I cranked the valve shut, and lay back in the steam to soak my hurts away.

I had quit the lawman trade, and yet I still thought like a peace officer. There in the dim light of the bath house my mind went back over the previous day's events and asked a lawman's questions.

Did a rustler problem *really* exist? Billie had missing cows and calves, as many as forty pairs. I had combed the range for C Heart stock and had come up empty. So had Kip Merriday, or at least that's what he said. Were rustlers the problem, or had Billie's cows merely strayed? And if there *were* stock thieves working the range, were they just a few long-rope artists and hungry homesteaders? Or was there an organized gang?

I slid down to my ears in the water and felt its heat ease away the pain in my neck. Well, I thought, Ross Devlin sure seems to think we're dealing with a gang. He's hired a posse of man hunters to deal with the situation.

I closed my eyes. There was one thing more. The rope-and-ring man I saw just before Devlin and his posse rode up had seemed *familiar* somehow.

I didn't catch a clear view of his face, but I could swear I'd seen his black hat and checkered

shirt someplace. I wasn't paid to play guessing games, and I wasn't sure enough to say anything to Billie, but the man I saw bore a strong resemblance to a feller we both knew—her former cowpuncher, Kip Merriday.

By the time I made my way over to the main house for supper, I was clean as spring water and loose as ashes. My neck and jaw still hurt considerable, but I felt enough better to believe I might someday be free of pain. It was that time of day when dusk lays over the land like a blanket and trees and brush huddle black in the twilight. Only the sky, empty of clouds and smooth as satin, held onto what leftover light there was.

I cleaned my boots on the scraper at the front door and stepped inside. The entryway was a catch-all of coats, saddle slickers, and headgear of various kinds and styles. I hung my hat on an empty peg and stepped up the stairs and into the kitchen. Billie sat unsmiling in her usual place at the table, a cup of coffee in her small hands. Maggie stood in her apron at the stove, her mouth a taut line. She looked as though she'd been crying. Clem Guthrie sat at Billie's right hand, his face red and his eyes flashing with an inner fire. I hadn't seen such a glum-looking outfit since one summer back home when the saloon ran out of beer.

I nearly asked *Who died?* but thought better of

it. Maybe somebody *had* died. Instead, I put on a friendly face and smiled. "Evenin'," I said, except the word came out sort of hoarse and raspy. Getting hanged by the neck does little to improve the sound of a person's voice.

Billie lifted her eyes to mine. She smiled a fragile smile. "Evening, Merlin," she said. "Looks like the gang's all here."

I looked around for the Baker twins. Billie read my mind. "I gave Jake and Alex their time this morning," she said. "They've gone home to their folks on Sage Creek."

Billie's smile faded. "They'll be back to help with the branding in a week or so. That is, if I'm still here in a week or so."

Clem Guthrie slammed his hand down on the table. "You'll be here, by grab!" he said. "If that damned bank tries to take the C Heart they'll have to go through me!"

Maggie turned away from the stove. "Hush, you old fool!" she said. "The bank will do whatever it *wants*. There's not a thing you can do about it."

Billie's hand touched the table top beside her. "Sit down, Merlin," she said. "You might as well join our merry little group."

I did as she asked, taking my place next to her. "You sure I should be part of this powwow?" I whispered.

"I should have told you before. The bank in Fairfax holds the mortgage on the C Heart. My

annual payment is past due, and I can't raise the money."

Billie stared into her coffee cup as though she could read the future there. "I'm going into Fairfax tomorrow. I'll ask for a six-month extension, but I don't think there's much hope."

I wanted to ask her why, but I decided it was not my place to do so. Again, Billie read my mind. "I have forty pairs missing. Cattle prices are down. I've tightened my belt to the last notch, but I still can't make that payment.

"What I *need* to do is buy more cattle and hire a full crew, but chances of the bank going with me on that are slim to none."

This time I didn't hesitate. "How come?" I asked. "Seems it would be in the bank's best interest to help you make a go of the place."

"You'd think so," Billie agreed. "But I'm afraid the bank doesn't see it that way."

My jaw was hurting again. I brushed my face with my fingertips. "Is there a dentist in Fairfax?"

"Why, yes," Billie said. "Doc Whitman. He has an office above the bank. Are you in pain?"

"Some. Mind if I ride in with you tomorrow?"

Billie smiled. "Not at all. I'd be glad for the company."

She pushed back her chair and stood up. Turning to Maggie, she said, "Now stop your sniffling and serve this cowboy the 'broken jaw soup' I promised him. We're not whipped yet!"

Maggie filled a soup bowl from a kettle on the stove and set it before me. "If you'll just get out of my way I'll be *glad* to serve him," she said. "Honestly!"

"*Honestly* is my favorite way of bein' served," I said.

Maggie's soup was hot and tasty, and I took in my fill of it. We spoke no more of mortgages and banks, remarking instead on neutral subjects like range conditions and the weather. Our small talk was a sham, of course, and we all knew it. Our palaver came in short bursts that were followed by long silences. Worries about the future of the C Heart ran like a cold current through our minds.

When supper was over, I thanked Maggie for her broken jaw soup and took my bowl and eating tools to the counter. Billie favored me with her wistful smile and said, "We'll head in to Fairfax in the morning right after breakfast. I need to pick up some supplies at the mercantile while we're there, so we'll take the wagon."

"I'll run the team in first thing," I said. "They'll be hitched and ready when you are."

Billie's smile lost its wistful cast and came on bright as bird song. "Good night, Merlin," she said. "I'll see you in the morning."

I gave her a smile back. "I don't see how you can keep from it," I said. "Good night, all."

The C Heart work team consisted of a pair of Belgian-Morgan horses, one a gelding and the other a mare. Billie called them Jack and Jill, and they were as stylish and steady as a person could ask for. I ran them in from the south pasture an hour before sunup and brushed and grained them at the barn. Clem ambled in and commenced to help me with the harness, but it appeared his mood hadn't improved much overnight. He was red-eyed and ringy, and he looked as rumpled and out-of-sorts as a wet owl.

"God *damn* a banker," he muttered. "Money-grubbin' som' bitches, every one."

I made no answer, but that didn't stop Clem.

"You take care of that girl today," he said. "Billie is fine and honest and true—everything E.B. Fairfax ain't—and she don't deserve to be took advantage of by that nickel-nursin' bean counter!"

"Fairfax?" I asked. "Same name as the town?"

Clem's hands trembled as he adjusted the rings of Jack's breeching.

"Hell *yes,* same as the town! Greedy som'bitch puts his name on *everything,* except maybe a half dozen *babies* he's sired around the county!

"Whenever some good-lookin' widow can't make her payment old E.B. likes to *console* her some before he forecloses on her house!"

"I'm beginnin' to get the impression you don't much *like* the man," I observed.

125

"I *don't,* by grab! I wouldn't *pee* on E.B. Fairfax if he was on *fire!*"

"Well," I said, "I recommend you calm down some before you work yourself into a heart attack. I have a feelin' the boss lady can take care of herself. And *nobody's* goin' to do her harm while *I'm* with her."

Clem backed off from a rolling boil to a simmer. "Oh hell," he said. "I know that. Just see you stay close to her while you're in town, you hear?"

"Close as her shadow," I said. "Now let's wash up and go to breakfast. You don't want to get on Maggie's bad side, do you?"

"Hell," Clem said. "I've *been* on Maggie's bad side for fifteen years."

We stepped out of the barn just as the sun took its first careful squint from behind the mountains. Up at the house, Maggie set the ranch triangle to clanging.

After chuck, I walked with Billie from the house to the wagon. She was dressed in riding boots, a heavy woolen skirt, and a tailored green jacket over a blouse of white silk. A pale green scarf was loosely knotted at her throat, and a pearl gray *sombrero* crowned her honeybrown hair. She wore kid gloves and carried a leather briefcase, and she held her head high. Since I'd met her, she had never looked so beautiful or seemed so brave.

I helped her up into the wagon's seat and

walked around to take the reins. She took my measure with a thoughtful glance and observed, "You're *still* not wearing a gun."

I smiled. "I understood we were going to the bank for a *meetin'*, not a *robbery*." Stepping up into the wagon, I took my place beside her. "But there is a Winchester in a scabbard behind you in the wagon box, in case you change your mind."

Billie laughed, and I was pleased my simple jest had taken away her worry, if only for a moment. "Thoughtful of you to bring it along," she said. "A person never knows when they might need to shoot a banker."

The road to Fairfax passed through rolling hills and across open stretches of grassland and sage under a sky that made a man's biggest plans seem small. Clouds drifted overhead and cast fast-moving shadows on the plains. Scrub cedar and jack pine crowned the hills, and flat-topped buttes reared up in the distance like steamboats on a sea of grass. Sitting on the wagon's spring seat beside Billie and breathing in the clean air of early morning gave me a feeling that the world was new and anything I dreamed was possible. For the first time since I left Miles City, I forgot my troubles and the ghost that haunted me.

I forgot about Ross Devlin and his *pistoleros*, too, although I had plenty of reason to recall them. The threat of rustlers working in the Big

Open vanished from my mind as well. I even forgot about Billie's troubles with the bank and her mortgage on the C Heart.

And then a cloud blocked the sun and we drove the road in its shadow. The day was fresh and pleasant in the sunlight, but the wind in shadow gave it a bitter chill. Worry came back like an unwelcome guest. There was trouble coming. I could feel it in my bones.

The town of Fairfax lay seventeen miles south of Billie's ranch on the banks of the Powder. Once a stage stop for coaches between Miles City and Deadwood, the town had come into being as a center for area ranchers and homesteaders. The stage still stopped there, but now a score of frame buildings stood where only the station and barn had been before. Wide, and shining like a ribbon in the sunlight, Powder River formed a backdrop for the town and its enterprises. I slowed the horses to a walk as we turned onto the main street.

The Fairfax Bank and Trust occupied a prominent spot at the intersection of Main and River Streets, directly across from a white-painted two-story building whose sign identified it as The Grand Hotel. Two stories high like its neighbor, the bank's first floor was devoted to the business of banking. From the signs on the windows facing the street, the second floor was devoted to the

offices of Wilson Mattingly, Attorney at Law, and A.J. Whitman, Painless Dentist.

"There's a decent restaurant at the hotel," Billie said. "We've time for a bite to eat if you're interested."

I drew rein outside the hotel's raised gallery. "I'm a talented eater," I said. "I'd make eating my *profession* if I could find someone who'd pay me to do it. But the truth is my jawbone is troublin' me a good deal more than somewhat. Maybe I'll just have a cup of coffee and watch *you* eat."

Billie's hearty laugh was my reward. Once again, I had lightened her spirits on a day when worry lay heavy on her mind. I was pleased with myself beyond measure.

"You certainly *are* devoted to eating," she said, laughing, "if you take pleasure in simply watching *others* do it!"

I'd take pleasure in watching you do anything, I thought.

What I said was, "That's a fact. If I can't *participate,* I'll be a *spectator*. It's better than nothing."

Then, just as it had on the road to Fairfax, the moment changed. Again, it seemed that a cloud blocked all the sunshine and light in the day and turned the world cold. Ross Devlin stepped through the doorway of the hotel and saw us. He smiled, his teeth white as mountain snow, and doffed his hat.

"Billie!" he said. "What a pleasant surprise! What brings you to the big city?"

That was just plain foolishness, I thought. Fairfax was neither big nor a city. Devlin was just trying to say something clever to impress Billie. I knew that was what he was doing because I did it myself.

"Hello, Ross," Billie said. "Just running a few errands. We were about to have dinner. What about you?"

Devlin glanced at me and his smile lost some of its brightness. He nodded, his face the very image of sincerity. "Fanshaw," he said. "I owe you an apology for that unfortunate incident the other day. I'm afraid my men and I jumped to a wrong conclusion."

"Too bad you couldn't stay for the party," I said. "Things *really* got unfortunate after you left."

"So I understand. Again, I'm sorry."

Devlin turned his attentions back to Billie. "See here," he said. "I'd like to take you both to dinner as a gesture of good will. What do you say?"

Billie hesitated, looking at me. "Merlin?"

I looked into Billie's eyes. She was allowing me to decide. I could tell Devlin no, turn him down flat. I surely had that right. But I wondered—would I look prideful and small in Billie's eyes if I did?

Sometimes I don't know what I'm going to do

until I've done it. I had told Clem Guthrie I'd stay as close to Billie as her shadow, but when push came to shove I just couldn't sit down with Ross Devlin.

I smiled at Billie. "I'm not all that hungry," I said. "You two go ahead. I think I'll see the dentist and then pick up your order at the mercantile. I'll be back here in an hour."

"All right," Billie said. "I'll meet you at the bank."

Turning away from the hotel, I looked up at the window of the dentist's office across the street. I couldn't help wondering if Doc Whitman could make *my* teeth as white as Devlin's.

Ten

THE WHOLE TRUTH

An outside wooden staircase led to the second floor of the Fairfax Bank building, and I took the steps two at a time just to work off some of my mad. At the top, a paneled door opened into a long hallway. I stepped inside and made my way down the corridor.

I smelled the dentist's office before I saw it. That rubbery, antiseptic smell, combined with a touch of cloves and mint, stays in a person's memory forever once he's had a whiff of it. The sign on the frosted glass of the door read the same as the window: *A.J. Whitman, Painless Dentist.* I turned the knob and went inside.

A white-haired gent in a boiled shirt and bow tie sat in the dentist's chair, reading a copy of the *Police Gazette.* He looked at me over the tops of his spectacles and asked, "Help you, cowboy?"

"Hope so. You Doc Whitman?"

"I am," he said, getting up from the chair. "What can I do for you?"

"I had my bell rung pretty good the other day. My back teeth are loose, and my jaw feels like maybe it's broke."

"Sit down," he said. "Let's have a look."

The doc had me open my mouth wide as I could and prospected around inside for awhile. If he was a "painless" dentist, I'd sure hate to have to deal with the other kind.

When he finally let up on me, Doc Whitman poured water in a basin and washed his hands. I couldn't help but wonder why he hadn't done that *before.*

"Good news," said the doctor. "Your jaw is not broken. You have a nasty bruise and some swelling, but there's no fracture.

"No real damage to your teeth, either. They are a bit loose, but they should firm up in a week or so."

I stood up. "Much obliged, Doc. What do I owe you?"

"Four bits ought to cover it. That's for the examination, and my professional recommendation."

"Which is?"

"Don't get hit in the jaw again."

I fished a half dollar from my pants pocket and handed it to him. "That's good advice," I said, "but my trail is strewn with hazards, and life is uncertain. I make no promises."

The horses were asleep in the sunlight when I came back from the dentist's office. I stepped up into the wagon's seat and shook the reins to rouse them. Jill came awake with a gentle flutter of ear and lip, while Jack awoke with a jerk, seemingly

embarrassed at being caught napping. I turned the team away from the hotel and rattled up the street toward the Fairfax Mercantile.

I drove toward the river, noticing the stores and shops along the way. At the Fairfax Feed Store, a woman in faded calico sat waiting on the seat of a sodbuster's work wagon. A balding merchant in a vest and sleeve protectors swept the boardwalk in front of the Fairfax Hardware. Two old-timers warmed their bones on the loafer's bench at the barber shop, and two plump ladies in sunbonnets came out of the Fairfax Dry Goods Store and crossed the street before me. I gave them a nod and tipped my hat as I drove by. I recalled Clem Guthrie's rant on how E.B. Fairfax had his name on most every business in town; Clem had not exaggerated, at least not by much. E.B. Fairfax seemed to be the bamboo chief in these parts, and he sure was proud of his name.

A dozen saddle horses stood loose-tied at the hitch rack in front of the Mint Saloon. Well, I thought, that's one business that doesn't have the Fairfax name attached to it. Out of habit, I read the brands as I passed. Nine out of the twelve horses wore the Rafter D. As I drew abreast of the bat-wing doors, I saw a group of men outside on the gallery. The saloon's board awning shaded the men, but I recognized three of them at once— Sam Bodie, cow boss of the Rafter D and the man who strung me up to a cottonwood; Maddox, the

long-haired gunman; and my former co-worker at Billie's place, Kip Merriday!

Bodie recognized me. I saw him frown, his square jaw grown tight. Still looking at me, he elbowed Maddox and said something that caused the gunman to look at me with new interest. Maddox had been in the act of rolling a smoke; now Merriday struck a match and held it for the gunman's cigarette. *Still making bad choices,* I thought. *Kip hankers to be a gunman and a killer, and now he's running with the real McCoy.*

Bodie's grin turned wolfish. Taking hold of the tails of his neck scarf, he raised his arm, his eyes bulging and his tongue stuck out like a hanged man. He nudged Maddox again and laughed. Maddox and Kip laughed, too. My hands tightened on the reins and became fists. My heart commenced to race; I felt the pulsing in my clenched jaw. I wanted to jump down and light into the three of them, but of course I did not. My Pa had been a fighting man. He enjoyed scrapping with other men and he seemed to have a talent for it. I remembered Pa's advice: *Keep your head. Never fight a man the way he wants to fight you.* I met their hot eyes with my own, and drove on up the street. There would be another time.

The storekeeper at the mercantile seemed nervous. "I'm Merlin Fanshaw," I said. "I ride for

the C Heart. Billie sent me by to pick up her order."

The man nodded, but he would not meet my eyes. "Yeah," he said. "Clem Guthrie said someone would be by," he said. "Mineral supplement and salt block for her cows, two rolls of barbed wire, a sack of oats, and five gallons of coal oil."

"That's right. Billie said to put it on her bill. I've got a wagon out front."

The storekeeper licked his lips. He raised his eyes to mine and looked quickly away. "I'm sorry, cowboy," he said, "but I can't help you. Miss Hart already owes me a considerable amount. I can't allow her any more credit until she pays her bill."

"I expect she'll pay you when she ships her calves," I said. "Isn't that when most ranchers settle their accounts?"

"From what I hear, Miss Hart might be goin' *out* of the cow business."

"That's news to me. You'd have to ask *her* about that."

"Yes. Well, that's what I heard."

"I'll be back, pardner," I said. "I'll bring Billie with me."

Billie was just leaving the bank as I pulled up in the wagon. A pigeon-chested gent in striped trousers and a black frock coat was escorting her out through the front door, and I surmised he

must be E.B. Fairfax, the boss banker himself. I stepped down and gave the gent a closer look.

For a man who had his name on most everything in town, Fairfax didn't appear to be all that much. Reading him from the top down, his hair was black as ink, aided somewhat by boot polish or hair dye. Neatly trimmed and parted down the middle, its youthful color didn't go with his near sixty-year-old face. Gold-rimmed spectacles made his careful gray eyes look bigger than they really were. Beneath a hooked nose, a well-groomed handlebar mustache graced his upper lip. Add to that a cruel mouth, teeth like white kernels on a corn cob, a weak chin, and the beginnings of a pot belly and you pretty much know what the man looked like.

Billie saw me and smiled. I tried to read her face for an answer regarding her extension, but I could not. Fairfax still held Billie's arm; he was looking at me, too.

"Hello, Merlin," Billie said. "You're right on time."

She turned to the banker. "This is my top hand at the C Heart, Merlin Fanshaw. Merlin, meet Ezra Fairfax, president of the bank."

Fairfax gave me a careless glance, but did not offer his hand. "Fanshaw," he said.

He turned back to Billie. "Again, Billie, I'm sorry. I honestly wish I could grant your request, but . . ." His shoulders lifted toward his stiff white

collar and dropped. He showed her the palms of his hands.

So the answer was no. Billie stood tall, her head high. I wanted to cheer. "I understand, Ezra," she said. "You have a duty to your depositors. I do thank you for seeing me."

I recalled our jest earlier that day about holding up the Fairfax Bank. For a wild half second, I thought about how E.B. Fairfax would look if I pulled the Winchester out of the wagon and threw down on him. Then I imagined myself taking hold of his coat lapels and shaking him like a terrier shakes a rat. I would not actually have done either of those things, but it was a pleasure just thinking about them.

I gave Billie a hand up into the wagon and took my place beside her. I hated to bring her more bad news, but there was no way around it.

"I drove up to the mercantile to pick up those supplies," I said, "but the storekeeper . . . well, he said he couldn't let you have them until you paid your bill."

Billie lowered her eyes. "So that's how it is," she said. "All right, let's go home."

"See here, Billie," I said. "I have a little money put aside. I got lucky awhile back at a poker game over in Butte. If you need a loan or anything . . ."

Billie smiled. She looked at me with a sort of wonder in her eyes. "You're really something, Merlin Fanshaw! Most cowhands would be

worried about getting their wages . . . or about being laid off. But you're offering to lend me *money!*

"I appreciate your offer, but I can't accept it. Besides, I still have enough cash to operate for a month or two. And we can get by without those supplies for a few weeks."

I made no reply, but turned the team away from Fairfax and onto the road to the ranch. I felt like we were being run out of town, and I didn't much like the feeling. Setting my face to the road ahead, I held my tongue and concentrated on my driving.

Billie shifted her position on the wagon seat. I felt her eyes on my face. "You haven't asked how my dinner with Ross went," she said.

I shrugged. "That's none of my business. I'm just a hired hand."

Billie smiled a wistful smile. "You're a good deal more than that, Merlin. So . . . you aren't curious?"

"I never said *that,* Billie. I said it's none of my business."

"Well, suppose I *wanted* to tell you. Would you let me?"

Sometimes talking to a woman makes a man feel like he's fighting bees. I could think of nothing to say, so that is what I wound up saying.

Apparently *no* answer was the *wrong* answer. Billie looked at me through half-closed eyes and

raised her voice a notch. "Well?" she said. "*Would* you?"

I turned the team off to the side of the road and drew rein. Shifting in the seat, I said, "Yes, Billie. If you want to tell me, I'll be plumb happy to listen."

"Ross Devlin offered to lend me the money to make my bank payment. I told him no."

I was glad to hear she'd turned him down, but I didn't feel it was my place to say so. Again, I didn't know what to say, so I said nothing.

"Why do you think I turned him down?"

I was tired of feeling like I had to watch my words. I looked into Billie's pretty brown eyes. "I think you figured accepting his loan would just mean you'd have *two* debts to pay instead of one. And you weren't sure what sort of *interest* Devlin might expect."

"My!" she said. "You *can* speak plainly when you put your mind to it. What else do you think?"

"I think you're either havin' the worst run of luck since Job or somebody's tryin' to run you off your place. Is that plain enough?"

"Yes," she said, her face serious now. "Plain enough."

For a time, Billie was silent. A fresh breeze riffled the tall grass alongside the road. Somewhere out in the sagebrush a meadowlark sang its bright song. Jack and Jill shifted in their traces.

"You know something of my dad's story," Billie said. "But you don't know it all.

"I told you about him the day we met. I told you he was something of a dreamer. Well, he surely was that. Calvin Hart, my dad, was a risk taker, a player of long odds, and a plunger. He was full of grand ideas and he saw possibilities in everything.

"Everybody liked Calvin. And Calvin liked everybody. But five years ago when he lost my mother, he began to ride out alone of a morning, sometimes staying out on the range all day. More and more, the ranch work fell on Clem Guthrie and me. Dad began to spend his nights in Fairfax, playing faro at the Mint. The saloon provided whiskey and companionship of a sort. I guess bucking the tiger appealed to the risk taker in him."

Billie fell silent again. Far out on the plains, cattle grazed. High overhead, a hawk carved lazy circles against the sky. I waited. Then Billie spoke again, and her voice sounded strained and tight.

"Then one night, Dad left the Mint and was headed home on his favorite saddle horse, Lucky Jim. No one knows exactly what happened—maybe Dad had too much to drink, maybe he stepped down in the darkness and then tried to mount again—but somehow his foot got caught in the stirrup and he lost control of Lucky Jim.

"A kid herding the town milk cows found him just after sunup two miles from town. Lucky Jim stood, cut up and lathered, against a homesteader's fence. Dad was dead, his left foot still in the stirrup. He'd been dragged to death."

Billie narrowed her eyes, looking out over the plain as if seeing the scene in her mind. I was turned toward her on the wagon seat, but she didn't look at me. She paused for a moment, and then spoke again.

"It was after his funeral that I learned the truth. Dad had mortgaged the C Heart to the hilt to pay his gambling debts. I inherited the ranch and the mortgage. I learned that Dad also owed nearly six thousand dollars to Milt Cosgrove, owner of the Mint Saloon, in gambling debts. Milt held Dad's IOUs."

Billie met my eyes and smiled a wry smile. "The other thing I inherited is Dad's bad luck," she said. "A few hard winters and dry summers and a year or two of low cattle prices left me cash poor and scratching. Then this spring those forty pairs went missing and it appears rustlers are working the Big Open. I keep trying to make ends meet, but hard luck keeps moving the ends.

"You've become a top hand and a friend," she said. "But to mix a metaphor, you may be a sailor on a sinking ship. I felt you needed to know the whole truth."

142

"So now I can jump ship and swim for shore?" I reached out and took her hand. "Much obliged, but I won't do that. I ride for the *brand.*"

Besides, I thought, *I'm not sure I know the whole truth yet.*

Eleven

A FRIEND IN NEED

Clem Guthrie was waiting for us when I drove the team over the bridge and reined up at the barn. I saw him glance at the rear of the wagon and then look at Billie's face before he turned his attention to me. There were questions in his eyes. *Where are the supplies? What about the extension on the bank loan?*

He offered his hand. Billie took it and stepped down. "You didn't ask," she said, "but I can see you're dying to know. Ezra Fairfax turned down my request for an extension. And we didn't pick up the supplies because the Mercantile won't give me any more credit. Does that about cover your questions?"

Clem's face flushed red. "*Damn,* Billie," he said. "I'm sorry, girl."

Billie relented. She smiled, and touched Clem's arm. "Me, too, old friend," she said. "But we'll get through this. We've seen tough times before."

Clem looked at me. "What about you, Merlin?" he asked. "You figure to drift?"

"Not just yet. Like I told Billie, I ride for the brand."

Clem grinned. "By grab, I *knew* you'd stick,"

he said. "Dam' if you ain't near as loco as the rest of us!"

I shrugged. "I've known some tough times myself. My pa used to say, 'It's *hell* when it's like this—and it's like this *now.*' "

"That just about sums it up," Clem said.

Watching us that night at supper, a stranger would have thought we didn't have a care in the world. Maggie served a fine meal of roast beef, potatoes, and gravy. Clem told stories of old times remembered, and I kept the ladies laughing with tales of my pa's wilder adventures. We said nothing about the bank's turndown or the C Heart's bill at the mercantile. Expressions of worry were banned by unspoken agreement, and self pity of any sort was strictly forbidden. I described, with many a quip and gesture, my visit to the dentist in Fairfax, and Clem told a big windy about a cowboy who had a tooth that was so bad the dentist had to amputate his head.

Later, we said good night and went our separate ways. Maggie and Billie washed and dried the dishes. Clem put an edge on the axe and split some firewood for the kitchen. I went down to the barn to tend the horses. On my way back to the bunkhouse, I stopped awhile to watch the stars come out. I heard the nighthawk's cry and listened to the frogs along the creek.

I thought about the events of the day, of Billie's

troubles and my own. Billie was between a rock and a hard place. She needed to buy more cattle and hire more cowhands in order to make the C Heart a paying proposition, but she couldn't finance the shirt-tail outfit she had, and the only cowhands on her payroll were Clem and me.

I recalled the men I'd seen at the Mint Saloon that afternoon. I remembered Sam Bodie's hot eyes and the wordless way he'd mocked me. Maddox, the gunman, had laughed at Bodie's jibe, looking at me with an expression of scorn on his hard face. Beside him, Kip Merriday stood in his shadow like an obedient sheepdog. Other of the big cattlemen's hired guns had been there as well, armed to the teeth and looking for trouble.

I had heard of no further action by the "regulators" but there was a tension in the air a man could almost smell.

Over the next few days, Clem and me made a last big gather and moved the C Heart heifers and their calves to fenced pasture near the home place. Except for the missing forty pairs, Billie had come through the winter with relatively few losses. The Rafter D and the other big outfits would soon be sending their riders and wagons out on spring roundup, but this year the C Heart would not be joining them.

Some small operators sent one of their riders to work the roundup as a rep, but Billie had decided to brand her calves at the home place and turn

them out to summer on open range. She would, that is, if she could find the money to keep going. Neighbors would offer their help—that was the way of ranch folk—but Billie would still require operating capital, and that would come only if the bank renewed her loan.

Billie's troubles were strong on my mind a few days later when Ross Devlin rumbled across the bridge in his side-sprung buggy and drew rein at the house. I'd been helping Clem with his chores and had stepped out into the sunlight just as Devlin drove in.

Ross got down from the buggy and smiled. "Morning, Merlin," he said. "Is Billie at home? I have some good news for her."

I nodded, stepping aside from the doorway. "Howdy, Ross," I said. "I reckon Billie could *use* some good news. She's in the kitchen with Maggie."

Uncertainty crossed Ross's face. "Much obliged," he said. "But my boots are muddy. Might be better if we meet outside. Would you let her know I'm here?"

"You bet," I said, and went back inside.

When I entered the kitchen, I saw that Billie had walked over to the front windows and was looking out at Ross's horse and rig. Maggie sat at the table, a cup of coffee before her. She was rolling a cigarette, but her hands trembled and she was having a hard time of it.

Speaking to Billie, I said, "Ross Devlin's outside. I asked him in, but he said he'd wait out front. Doesn't want to track mud in your house."

Billie turned away from the windows and walked toward the short stairway that led down to the front door. Passing Maggie, she said, "Ross is *afraid* to come in. He thinks you don't like him."

Maggie's face was hard as flint. "I wonder what gave him *that* idea," she said.

I followed Billie downstairs, but stayed behind her in the vestibule. Ross beamed when Billie opened the door and stepped outside.

"Good morning, Ross," she said. "Please—come in."

Ross looked up at the front windows, and then back into Billie's eyes. "Thank you, Billie," he said, "but I can't stay. I have good news for you, and wanted to let you know.

"After you left town the other day, I ran into Ezra at the bank. He told me you'd asked for a six-month extension of your loan, and that he'd had to turn you down."

"He told *you?* Nice to hear he's keeping our business confidential."

"Ezra's an old friend. Turning you down was difficult for him."

"As it was for me. All right. What's the good news?"

Ross smiled. His smile had lost none of its dazzle. "I talked him into giving you the

extension you asked for. Said I'd personally guarantee your payment."

Billie frowned. "Ross . . . I'm pleased about the extension, but I'm sorry you intervened. My troubles really aren't your concern."

"They *could* be," he said. "I could make them all go away."

"Please, Ross. That's old ground. You know I turned your loan offer down."

Ross nodded. "Pride," he said. "My talk with Ezra was only friendly persuasion on your behalf. I offer no loan. You incur no debt with me."

From my place inside the screen door, I saw Billie's resolve begin to crumble. Her shoulders slumped. Relief brought a tremor to her voice. "Thank you, Ross," she said. "And thank you for driving all the way out here to tell me."

Ross held Billie with his eyes. "Always my pleasure," he said. "Just stop at the bank when you're in town. Ezra will have the paperwork ready. He says he will also open a line of credit for operating expenses."

Ross flashed his big white-toothed smile and turned back to his waiting horse and buggy. Billie watched as he drove away.

And me? Well, I watched Billie watch Ross drive away.

Billie wasted no time. When Clem and me showed up for chuck the next morning, she was

dressed for town and chipper as bird song. "Going back to town today," she said. "Seems Ezra Fairfax has had a change of heart."

Clem frowned. He was surprised by Billie's announcement but trying hard not to show it. "I didn't think the old skinflint *had* a heart," he muttered.

"All right," Billie said. "Then let's say he had a change of *mind*. Heartless he may be, but nobody ever called him *mindless*."

Maggie brought a platter of hotcakes over from the stove and set them before us. Clem helped himself and stared at his plate. Maggie's mouth was a bitter line, and it sure didn't take a mind reader to know she was on the prod. Billie gave her a quick sideways glance. "Ross Devlin stopped by yesterday. Apparently, he talked Ezra into granting me an extension on my note, and a line of credit for expenses."

"Hell, you say," Clem said. "What does Devlin get out of it?"

Billie's brown eyes flashed. "Ross did me a favor out of friendship, no strings attached," she said. "I know you don't like him—and Maggie goes wall-eyed at the very mention of his name— but I'm trying to hold this place together. At this point, I'm not inclined to look a gift horse in the mouth!"

Clem looked down at the hotcakes on his plate and held his tongue. Maggie set the coffee pot

back on the stove with a bang, and plopped down on a chair by the wood box.

Billie turned to me with fire in her eye. "Well?" she said. "*Everybody* here seems to have an opinion. What do *you* have to say?"

Meek and mild as any lamb, I pointed toward the platter with my fork. "Pass the hotcakes," I said.

Billie laughed. Clem looked up from his plate and grinned. Even Maggie managed a smile. "All right," Billie said. "After breakfast we'll take the wagon into town. Merlin, I want both you and Clem to come with me. We'll pick up those supplies at the Mercantile after I've talked to the banker."

Clem slung a leg over the bench and stood up. "That suits me right down to the ground," he said. "When we get through loadin' them supplies, you reckon Merlin and me could have us a beer over at the Mint?"

Billie shook her head. "I don't know why not," she said. "I might even buy a round, if you behave yourselves. Now go hitch up the team while I'm still feeling generous."

Clem seemed as tickled as a kid going to a circus. After we ran Jack and Jill in and hitched them to the wagon, Clem washed up at the bunkhouse and changed from his dirty shirt to an almost clean one. "I'm fixin' to get me a barber shave and a haircut," he said. "By grab, I ain't

been to town since Billie fired that Ferriday kid."

"Appears to me you're gettin' pretty dandified for a workday trip to Fairfax. I'm thinkin' you've maybe got a lady friend in town."

Clem actually blushed. "Well, if I do, I ain't met her yet. But I am open and a-hopin'."

"*Open and a-hopin'* are good cards in the romance game," I said, "but a man needs *willin' and able* to win the pot."

"Two pair, huh? How about if I draw *ready, willin' and able*? That'd give me a full house—a winnin' hand in *any* man's game."

Twelve

A Close Shave

When we topped the last hill and turned the wagon onto Fairfax's main street it looked as if the entire population of the Big Open had come to town. Saddlehorses lined the hitch racks, and homesteaders' wagons stood outside the dry goods and grocery stores. I saw teamsters offloading crates and boxes, and watched a beer wagon pulled by four high-stepping Clydesdales come rumbling up the street.

Men and women crossed the dusty thoroughfare on foot, weaving their way through the horse-drawn traffic. I drew rein at the bank, and helped Billie down.

"Meet me at the hotel in an hour," she said. "We'll pick up those supplies and head back to the ranch."

Clem assumed a feisty look. "I still think I should go to the bank with you. If that money-grubbin' banker don't treat you right, I can whup on him for you."

Billie laughed. "You're some big talker, Clem Guthrie. If I need someone to stupefy the man with chin music, I may call on you."

We watched as Billie entered the bank. Clem

grinned, his face a riot of wrinkles. "Ain't she a pistol?" he said.

"If she's not, she'll do until a pistol comes along," I said.

We turned away from the bank and drove toward the livery stable at the end of the street. At the Mint Saloon, several Rafter D horses dozed at the hitch rail. Three or four waddies stood talking outside, but I can't say whether they were Ross Devlin's men or not. They raised their heads to watch us as we passed, and then went back to their talk.

Seeing the Rafter D horses reminded me of my last time in town. On that day, Devlin's men had watched me drive past, like wolves watching a sheep drive. Devlin's cow boss, Sam Bodie, had mocked me, making sport of my near hanging and leading the other men in laughter.

I figured I owed the man. Not only had he strung me up that day in the badlands above Mizpah Creek, but he'd clubbed me with his rifle butt and knocked me down. For the most part, I held no hard feelings against the riders who jumped me; circumstances sure had made me look guilty. But Sam Bodie hadn't seemed to care much whether I was innocent or not. He'd been out to hang somebody and I was handy. Now I'm as good natured as the next man, but being lynched for something I didn't do was a thing I tended to take *personal.*

"Where are we goin'?" Clem asked. "If you're takin' me on a tour of this ant hill, you needn't bother. I've already *saw* Fairfax."

And right then is when I saw Sam Bodie. The Rafter D cow boss stepped out of the Mint Saloon and squinted against the bright sunlight. Bodie looked directly at Clem and me but did not seem to recognize us. Then he hitched up his gun belt, pulled his hat down low over his eyes, and swaggered out into the street.

I watched Bodie cross to the other side and go into the barber shop. Seated there in the wagon seat, I felt my blood rise like sap in a sycamore, and I took a notion. Or maybe a notion took *me*.

I handed the reins to Clem and stepped down. "Wait for me," I said. "I'll be back directly."

Clem gave me a sharp look. "If you're thinkin' what I *think* you're thinkin'," he said, "there's a few things you should know. I've seen Sam Bodie fight, and he's rougher than a cob.

"Bodie's a big man, and he likes to use his weight to gain an edge. He'll come at you in a rush like a mad bull and try to knock you off your feet. Once he gets you on the ground, he'll make it mighty hard for you to get up. He'll put the boots to you and tromp you to a grease spot. Most of Bodie's fights don't last all that long."

"That's good," I said. "I don't have all day."

I looked back at Clem. "Do me a favor," I said.

"If any of that crowd at the Mint tries to draw cards in this game, *discourage* them."

"How am I supposed to do that?"

"There's a Winchester behind you in the wagon box. I don't have time to show you how to use it."

Sam Bodie was already laid back in the chair when I entered the barber shop. Draped with a cloth from neck to knees, a hot towel hid his face. The barber looked up from where he stood stropping his straightedge and said, "Welcome to Mel's barber shop, son. I'm Mel, and you're next."

"No," I said. "*He* is." And I whipped the cloth off Sam Bodie.

Eyes wide and staring, Bodie came up out of the chair fast. He grabbed for his holstered six-shooter, but my hand found it first and jerked it from the leather. As Bodie found his footing, I dodged and threw the gun out through the open door.

Bodie crouched, blocking my way. I turned, caught between the man and the shop's pot-bellied stove. As Clem predicted he would, Bodie lowered his head and charged. He was fast for a big man, but I was faster. Stepping to one side, I let him collide head first with the stove. The pot-belly rocked on its legs, breaking free of its stove pipe, and black soot dusted the room. I stepped in close and brought an uppercut from the floor into Bodie's face. Pain shot up my arm from the blow,

but Bodie kept a-coming. I sidestepped again, chopping at his head with a series of quick rights. I don't know whether it was my punches or Bodie's reckless rush, but the big man slipped and fell to his knees on the shop's linoleum floor.

Quick as a cat, he turned. He aimed a kick at my crotch, but I dodged and took his boot heel on my thigh. I tried to stay free of his grasp, but he got his hands on me and locked me in a bear hug. I couldn't breathe. I thought my back would surely break. Bodie's face was an inch from my own, his eyeballs bulging and his face red as fire. I smelled liver and onions on his breath, and decided he was close enough. I reared back and brought my head hard into his face. I felt his nose break, heard his roar of pain and fury loud in my ears. He rolled away, streaming blood, and struck the barber's cabinet with a crash.

Bottles toppled and crashed to the floor. Tools of the tonsorial trade—scissors, combs, razors, and such—clattered down as well. I caught a quick glimpse of the barber, who seemed mainly to be trying to avoid the fray. Bodie's hand closed on a straight razor and flicked it open. I ducked back as the blade caught sunlight and flashed by an inch from my face. I broke a bottle of hair tonic over Bodie's head, which caused him to drop the razor but didn't improve his hair none as far as I could see.

Bodie stunned me with a wild swing, which

sent me through the open door and onto the raised boardwalk. I felt like I'd been kicked by one of those beer wagon Clydesdales. I expect the barber was relieved to have us out of his shop before we destroyed it entirely, but I was not at all sure I had improved my situation. Bodie was coming fast, raising a foot to stomp me, and I felt that all things being equal, I druther not be stomped. I struck out with my own kick and heard Bodie's knee pop before I rolled out of his path.

I was on my feet before Bodie was on his. His knee had to be hurting him bad, but he lowered his head to make another run at me. This time I didn't dodge. Raising my arms high, I brought my clenched fists down on the back of Bodie's neck with everything I had. His big body went rag-doll limp, and then he fell face first to the boardwalk, struggled to his feet for a moment, and then toppled off the walk to the street below.

I was gasping like a catfish on a river bank. I could not get my breath. My heart was pounding like a jackhammer. I was dog tired and bone weary, but I still had one more chore to do. Bodie's six-gun lay in the street where I'd thrown it, glinting in the daylight. I bent over and picked it up. Just down from the barber shop stood a cast iron pump and a rough-hewn water trough. The trough was full almost to the brim. Working the ejector rod on Bodie's gun, I shucked its

cartridges. Then I snapped the loading gate closed and tossed the gun into the trough.

Bodie was trying to get to his feet, but he hadn't made it yet. Blood dripped from his broken nose. "Next time you go to hang a rustler," I said, "you might want to make sure he *is* one."

I looked up to see Clem watching from the wagon's seat, the Winchester in his hands. A crowd had begun to gather, including the riders I'd seen in front of the Mint, but nobody made a hostile move. I knocked the dust from my hat and put it on. Walking as straight and loose as I was able, I passed in front of the spectators and clumb up into the wagon with Clem.

Nobody said a word, but I noted that several of the cowhands gave me a thoughtful look as if they were revising their appraisal of me. One man tried to help Bodie to his feet, but the cow boss cussed him and pushed his hand away.

"For a man who don't pack a six-shooter," Clem said, "you're about half *war-like*."

After Bodie fished his gun from the trough and hobbled off with some of the Rafter D riders, Clem and me paid a call on the barber at his shop.

"Sorry about bustin' up your tonsorial parlor," I said. "Would ten dollars cover the damages?"

The barber grinned. "Hell, son," he said. "That's too much money. Make it five, and we'll call it square.

"Besides," he said, "I've got a feelin' I'll have

more business than ever now. You've made this place famous."

"How's that?"

"Sam Bodie likes to throw his weight around. A lot of men in this town are gonna want to have their ears lowered in the place where big Sam met his match."

"By grab, I'm one," said Clem, climbing into the barber chair. "I'll take a haircut and a close shave."

"No close shave for me," I said. "I think I just *had* one."

Thirteen

A BRANDING AND A BURNING

Mel the barber gave Clem a first-class haircut, mostly trimming up his side hair. Clem believed he still had hair on top, but he hadn't looked up there lately. The hairs in his top knot had fell away over the years like autumn leaves, and his scalp above the ears was mostly freckled skin. When the haircut was done the barber gave Clem a shave that left his weathered old face nigh as smooth as a baby's . . . well, as smooth as a baby. Then he turned his attentions to me.

After asking me to get in the chair, he went to work on my scrapes and scratches with carbolic acid and arnica and cleaned me up considerable. I knew I wouldn't pass Billie's sharp-eyed inspection, but at least I looked some better. We paid the man, told him we were much obliged, and set out to meet Billie at the hotel.

When we entered the hotel's lobby, Billie was sitting primly on the red plush circular sofa with her briefcase in her lap. She stood up when she saw us walking toward her.

"I didn't witness your scuffle with Sam Bodie," Billie said, "but at least three people so far have told me about it."

"What's the general verdict?" I asked. "Did I win, or lose?"

Billie smiled. "The jury's still out. From what I hear, you won the *first* round at least."

"Yes," I said. "Our set-to was brief, but I believe I got my point across."

"So I understand. Something about avoiding mistaken identity?"

"Pretty much," I agreed.

Clem chimed in, "It's a bad day for Goliath when little David gets a belly full."

Billie laughed. "Righteous wrath is a terrible thing," she said. "Let's go have that beer."

Back at the ranch, we gathered and branded Billie's calves. The big cow outfits did their branding on the open range, but we weren't as well-fixed for cowpunchers—or cows—as they were. We penned the C Heart's cattle in the pasture below the home place and branded in the big corral behind the barn. I did the roping, Jake and Alex Baker were flankers, or rasslers, and Clem and Billie tended the irons and branded.

The roper at a branding needs a steady horse and a steady hand. He first needs to make sure the calf is following its own mammy, and then he dabs a loop on the little critter and drags it to the fire. If the calves are small, the roper goes for a head catch. A head caught calf usually keeps his feet, pulling back but coming along because he

don't have much choice. One of the rasslers then flanks the calf and with his pardner lays it out for the iron. If the calves are bigger, the roper will catch them by the heels. This throws them and saves the rasslers the trouble of having to flank the animal. A good roper can keep three sets of rasslers busy. I only had to keep the Baker twins busy, so I had it pretty easy.

Clem did the knife work. He cropped ears and castrated the bull calves, and it was plain he'd done the job many a time before. Billie handled the irons, branding the C Heart with two separate irons and making sure the brand was applied clear and proper. Maggie even came down from the house and lent Billie a hand, keeping the irons hot but not *too* hot. We may not have had as big a crew as the open range outfits, but we made out all right.

When the branding was finished and the cows and calves were turned out to mother up and settle down, Clem and me joined the Baker twins for a bath in the creek. I could have used a good soak and scrub in the bath house, but Billie and Maggie already had dibs on that option. It was ladies to the bath house and gents to the creek, which everybody agreed was fair enough.

That evening, I sat out in front of the bunkhouse waiting for Maggie to ring the supper bell. Across the creek, cows and calves drifted easy along the ridge, backlit by the setting sun. A soft breeze

riffled the leaves of the cottonwoods and laid a cooling touch on my still-wet hair.

In that moment, I felt a peace I had not known for some time. The grief that tormented me after the shooting of Toby Slocum had not gone away—I supposed it never would entirely—but it had faded to a hollow ache a man could live with.

I rode for the C Heart. I was Billie Hart's top hand. I liked the familiar routines of the ranch. I liked working cattle. I liked Maggie, Clem, and the Baker twins. And I liked Billie. I liked Billie most of all.

I was happy for her. In spite of the missing cattle, Billie's calf crop was better than she expected. The bank in Fairfax had given her a six-month extension on her loan payment and a line of credit to boot.

As for Devlin's regulators, I'd heard nothing further about their rustler hunt since the day they jumped me above Mizpah Creek. Maybe they'd had second thoughts about using lynch law to solve their problems. Maybe the rustling problem was only a few long rope artists and nowhere near as serious as they'd believed.

And then I recalled the cold gray eyes of the man called Maddox and threw a check-rein on all my maybes. Maddox was a killer, pure and simple, and so were the men he led. Trouble was coming to the Big Open, trouble that would touch the lives of the people I'd come to know and care about.

As sure as God made sunsets and good horses, trouble would touch *my* life as well. There was no maybe to it.

Next morning, after chuck, the Baker twins saddled up the old work mare they called Shirley and bade us goodbye for the time being. Billie paid the boys their wages to date, and they were anxious to get back to their home on Sage Creek.

"The folks are a mite short of cash money at our place," Alex Baker said, "and Pa will be needin' Shirley here for spring plowin' soon."

"Shirley's a good natured old girl," I said. "She lets you boys ride her double, and pulls a plow for you, too."

Jake Baker grinned. "Yeah," she said. "Old Shirley ain't much for looks, but she's a hard worker."

I rubbed the mare's neck. "Same as you boys," I said. "Must run in the family."

Jake's grin widened. "Expect so," he said. Jake stepped up into the saddle. Taking his brother's arm, Alex swung up behind him.

"We'll be back day after tomorrow," Alex said. "Miss Billie says she wants to start cuttin' hay in that lower pasture."

"See you then," I said. "If I know Clem, he'll have the sickle sharp enough to shave with and the mowin' machine runnin' like a four-dollar watch."

"Expect so," Alex said. Then the boys turned

Shirley out toward the road that would take them to Sage Creek.

For just a moment, as I watched them ride away, I sort of wished I could be sixteen again myself.

It was just after chuck the next morning when I saw Alex again. He came thundering across the bridge on Shirley, whipping her both ways as he rode. The mare was not accustomed to hard running, but she was doing her best. Lather flecked her withers and flanks, and she wheezed like a bellows as she lumbered toward me. Judging by appearances, Alex must have run her all seven miles from Sage Creek.

I stepped out into his path and reached for Shirley's reins. "Hold up there, Alex," I said. "You know better than to use a horse that way!"

And then I had a good look at Alex. He was clad in a homespun nightshirt and faded waist overalls, and his straw-colored hair was as tangled as a magpie's nest. Smoke had stained his nightshirt, but also his face and hands. His eyes were wild and staring, and tears had washed clean tracks through the grime.

"Riders, Merlin!" Alex said. "They hit us last night! They burned our house and took my Pa!"

"Riders? Who . . ."

"I . . . I don't know! *Regulators,* maybe! That white-haired man—the one they call Maddox—

166

he was there! Maybe six or seven others . . . nobody I ever saw before. They said my pa was a *rustler!*"

I recalled the morning I met Irv Baker at his hard-luck farm. A used-up man with too much family and too little cash. Hope had burned low in his nervous eyes that day, and fear had held him like a trapped rat. I recalled the Durham steer's green hide on the corral fence and the man's sheepish look. "Ross Devlin allows us to butcher a steer now and again," he'd said.

Had Devlin changed his policy? Had Irv Baker gone beyond 'now and again'?

Shirley's wet sides heaved, steaming in the chill morning air. I held her reins as Alex stepped down.

"My ma, Merlin . . . she's beside herself! They made her take the young'uns outside—Sally, Ruthie, baby Luke—and then they set fire to the house! They made Pa get on our old saddle horse—and they took him away!"

"What about your brother Jake? Where is he?"

"Jake and me tried to put the fire out, but we couldn't—I left him to take care of Ma and the others while I rode back here! I didn't know what else to do."

"You did right," I said. "Put Shirley in the barn—we'll saddle a couple of fresh horses and go back to your place. Don't worry, boy—we'll find your Pa."

I turned and nearly ran into Billie. Seeing Alex

from the house, she had sensed trouble and had come out to learn its nature. Her expression was serious, her brown eyes sympathetic.

"I'll send Clem over with the wagon," she said. "We'll put your mother and the children up here for awhile. The family can stay at the bunkhouse."

"That's right," I said. "Clem and me will bed down in the barn."

Minutes later, I'd caught up my Rutherford horse and the gelding I called Roanie. I did not choose my own horses on purpose; it's just that they were the first I could catch. Inside the barn, I snugged down my saddle on Rutherford and watched Alex draw the cinch on a C Heart rig. When we led the horses outside, Clem was already hitching the team and Maggie was loading quilts and blankets into the wagon bed.

I slid the Winchester into the saddle boot and stepped up onto Rutherford. Billie glanced at the rifle, her face grave, and nodded. I gave back her nod, and with it my promise. I would do what I could for the Bakers.

Rutherford and Roanie had run together before. I touched the buckskin with my spurs and both horses struck out as one on the road to Sage Creek.

We saw the smoke first, a dark smudge staining the morning sky. Ahead lay the low hill that

marked the location of the Baker farm. Alex and me turned our horses off the road and swept around the hill's base. The family's sod-roofed home still burned, flames and smoke rising from its blackened timbers. Martha Baker and her children were gathered nearby.

I was struck by the scene. Bereft by misfortune, the forlorn family huddled close to the flames, taking warmth at least from a house that could offer them nothing else. Alex's twin brother, Jake, stood beside his mother, his father's short-barreled rifle in his hands. Seeing Alex and me riding in, he stepped quickly aside from the others and prepared to defend them.

"No, Jake," Alex called out. "It's me—me, and Merlin from the C Heart!"

Jake lowered the rifle. He watched us, his face begrimed by smoke and looking much older than his sixteen years. I reined Rutherford to a stop and stepped down. Mrs. Baker sat back away from the burning logs of the farmhouse in a rocking chair. She was still in her night dress, a black woolen shawl clutched about her slim shoulders. Her daughters, Sally and Ruthie, stood at their mother's side, one on her left and one on her right. The girl called Ruthie held Luke, the baby.

I doffed my hat. "Miz Baker, I'm Merlin Fanshaw. I ride for the C Heart. I work with your boys."

She looked up at me, her eyes red-rimmed from the smoke. She leaned forward, straining as if trying to understand my words. Tears flowed freely down her face. She said, "My husband ain't at home right now. Them men done *taken* him."

"Yes, ma'am. Alex told me. We're goin' to look for him."

"I'd be obliged," she said.

"Miz Baker," I said. "Lady I ride for, Billie Hart, is sendin' a wagon for you and the children. Clem Guthrie will take you all back to the C Heart for awhile. He'll be along directly."

She turned to her son, Jake. "What's this man sayin', Jakie?"

"It's all right, Ma," Jake said. "Miss Billie wants you to come to her house. For a visit, like. While we get things fixed up here."

I swallowed the lump in my throat and turned back to Alex. "Which way did those riders go?"

Alex pointed. "That way," he said. "Right through our garden."

Leading Rutherford, I studied the soft earth. The horses' hooves had carried wet clods of dirt beyond the garden and off into the hard-packed prairie beyond.

"The ground is hard as flint," I said, more to myself than to Alex. "I may not be the world's best tracker, but I've worked with the best. Hoodoo Hawks, drunk or sober, could track a

dragonfly over bedrock. And a former lady friend of mine, Pandora Pretty Hawk, is the best I ever saw. I learned from both of them. I'll find your Pa."

"*We'll* find him," Alex said. "I'm comin' with you."

Alex Baker was part boy and part man, but it was the man part that was talking. "He's my *Pa,* Merlin."

"All right," I said. "Get your hat and bring that short-barreled rifle. *We'll* find your pa."

Fourteen

IRV BAKER'S LAST RIDE

We found Irv Baker an hour's ride from his farm. Following the tracks of the raiders' horses, Alex and me broke out atop a sand rock ridge and drew rein, looking down at the valley below. At the foot of the slope that dropped away before us, a muddy stream snaked across the valley floor, bordered by brush and a grove of weathered cottonwoods. Above the trees and in their branches, magpies chattered and scolded.

I couldn't put my finger on it, but something about the scene didn't seem right. I narrowed my eyes, studying the grove, and that's when I saw the corpse. Irv Baker hung suspended by the neck from a cottonwood limb, his hands tied behind his back and his feet bound together with a pigging string. In that moment, I knew what had drawn the magpies' attention.

"*Pa!*" Alex shouted, and I knew the boy saw him, too. "*Pa!*" Alex shouted again, anger and grief giving an edge to his voice that hurt a man to hear. "God *damn* those men! God damn them to hell!" And he drove the roan hard down the slope.

I touched Rutherford's flanks with my spurs

and leaned back as the buckskin followed Alex downhill in a series of stiff-legged bounds. At the foot of the slope, I stared up at Irv's body and the sight burned a hole in my brain. Irv's head canted to the right, the rope taut at his throat. His face was flushed, a deep purple in color. Between broken teeth, his tongue protruded thick and swollen. And pinned to the front of his nightshirt was a handwritten sign that read: "Cattle Thief."

Alex threw himself from the saddle and ran to his father. I rode in close, stood in the stirrups, and flipped open my Barlow. "Catch him, Alex," I said. "Don't let him fall." Then I leaned out and cut the rope.

Alex braced himself, his feet apart, and grasped his father's corpse about the waist. The body's dead weight jack-knifed across his shoulder, and the boy staggered but kept his feet. Gently, he eased the body to the ground.

"Pa was no cow thief," Alex said. "Sure—we butchered a Rafter D steer now and then to feed our family, but Mister Devlin said we could."

Tears streamed down the boy's face as he gave in to his grief. "Can't . . . seem to keep from *bawlin',*" he said.

"Whoever told you a man don't *cry* now and again probably lies about other things, too," I said. "If a man can't cry when his pa dies, when *can* he?"

I left Alex alone with his father's body and took

to studying the ground. I found horse tracks, boot prints, and the like, but nothing else of interest until . . .

At my feet in the sandy loam beneath the cottonwood, I caught the glint of sunlight on metal. Stooping, I brushed the dirt away and picked up a cast-off spur rowel, a six-pointed steel star about an inch and a half in diameter. Examining the rowel, I asked myself the question I'd learned from Pandora and Hoodoo: *What does this tell you?*

Well, I thought, first of all this rowel probably *didn't* belong to any of the Texas gunmen I'd heard about. Most of the Texas boys used bigger rowels on their spurs, two inches or more in diameter. The rowel itself was usually of the long-pronged type. Cowhands on the northern range favored a small, short-pronged rowel on a two-inch shank, or maybe a five-pointed star.

Losing a rowel was not unusual on the range. Over time, the rivet that held the rowel fast wore down or broke, and a rider had to replace it. What *was* unusual was a rowel with a six-pointed star. I had never seen a six-pointed star rowel before. Of course, that didn't necessarily mean they were all that rare, just that *I* hadn't seen one. I looked at it again, listening for what it might tell me, and then tucked it away in the pocket of my vest.

It was when I turned back to Alex that I saw the horse. The animal stood, nervous as a spinster in

a bunkhouse, watching us from the brush along the creek. Goose-rumped and gotch-eared, the horse wore a well-used Denver saddle and an old work bridle with rope reins. Looking at Alex, I pointed out the horse with a nod of my head.

"That the saddlehorse you told me about?"

Alex nodded. "That's him, all right. Old Pokey. He gave Pa his last ride."

"*Next* to last. Catch him up. He can carry your pa into Fairfax."

Alex looked at me. "We takin' Pa to Fairfax? How come?"

"Two reasons," I said. "I expect the town has an undertaker. And some kind of lawman."

The boy nodded. "Peaceful Valley Mortuary on River Street," he said. "And City Marshal Casper Bentwood."

Alex shrugged. "Bentwood ain't *much* of a lawman, Merlin. Pap said he's useless as teats on a boar."

"That's as may be," I said. "But a mob has murdered a citizen, and we're duty bound to notify somebody who wears a star. By rights we should take him to the county sheriff at Miles City, but that's two days' ride, maybe three. We may wish Marshal Bentwood was a better man, but any old port in a storm, as the sailors say."

We loaded Irv Baker's body face down across Old Pokey's back and struck out for Fairfax. I took the lead and Alex brought up the rear, his

haunted eyes on the corpse that was his father. We were a sad procession, small and alone beneath an endless blue sky—Irv Baker's lifeless body, the noose still taut about his neck; Alex, smoke-stained and grieving, looking older than his sixteen years; and me, ex-deputy Merlin Fanshaw, a lawman no longer and feeling guilty somehow because I wasn't.

There were only a few people on the streets when we rode in, but those who were gave us their full attention. Up the street from the bank, the barber stood in the doorway of his shop, his face grave. As we rode past the mercantile, a plump woman with a toddler in tow looked up suddenly and quickly covered the child's eyes with her hand. At the Mint Saloon's hitch rack, a cowhand paused in the act of untying his horse and watched us pass without expression.

The city marshal's office occupied a weed-filled lot at the end of the street, and it was there we drew rein. In the deep shadow of the board awning, a dough-bellied man with bulldog jowls stood watching.

"What's that you got there, son?" he asked.

"I'm lookin' for the city marshal," I said.

"You're talkin' to him," he said. "Casper Bentwood, City Marshal, night watchman, and notary public. I asked what you got there."

"Dead man name of Irv Baker. He had a little

place up on Sage Creek. That's his boy, Alex, on the roan."

Marshal Bentwood stepped into the light, shielding his eyes from the sun. "And who might you be?"

"Merlin Fanshaw. I ride for the C Heart. Night riders took Baker from his family last night and burned his house. Alex and me found him hangin' from a cottonwood limb this mornin'."

Bentwood shrugged. "I heard some of the big outfits are cleanin' out the rustlers in the county. *Might* be your friend Baker was a cow thief."

"*Might* be a pig can play a banjo, but I doubt it. Last I heard, lynchin' was *illegal.* What the hell kind of lawman *are* you, Bentwood?"

"The *city* kind, son. My jurisdiction ends at the city limits. This appears to be a matter for the county. You need to talk to Tom Irvine, up at Miles City."

I shook my head. "Yes," I said. "I suppose I do. I can't *tell* you how much I appreciate your help and advice."

As I turned back to Alex and the horses, I said, "I may call on you again sometime . . . if I need somethin' *notarized.*"

We had a better reception at the funeral parlor. Archie Grimsrud, the undertaker there, had practiced sympathy for so long he almost made Alex feel he'd been Irv Baker's personal friend.

While Alex poured out his heart to the man, I made it clear we were willing and able to pay for the dearly departed's final send-off, but only at the lowest possible price. These delicate negotiations took place through words and gestures between Grimsrud and me, of which Alex was entirely unaware.

As Alex was finishing up the paperwork, I helped the undertaker's assistant carry Irv's body downstairs to the work room. When I came back upstairs, I drew Alex aside.

"I have to run a few errands," I said. "Wait for me here; I'll be back directly." The boy seemed bewildered and lost, but after a long pause he looked me in the eye and nodded his understanding. I stepped outside, swung up onto Rutherford, and set off for the heart of town.

I figured the sign out front was meant to appeal to the Texas trail hands who had come north with the big herds and stayed on. "Lone Star Saddle Shop" the sign read, and when I walked inside I found it to be a saddle shop and something more. My nostrils caught the familiar smells of new leather, neats-foot oil, and saddle soap, and the shelves behind the sales counter were filled with all manner of leather goods and tack. Saddles for sale were displayed on stands. Saddlebags, chaps, bridles, harness, and scabbards hung from pegs on the wall. But the shop also carried

merchandise other than leather goods, as I thought it might. Saddle blankets, spurs, bridles, and lariats were on display and on the shelves. I figured a cowhand could find most everything he needed there if only he had the price.

I was still looking at the inventory when a slim hombre left the work room and came toward me. He wore high-topped boots and a big weathered Stetson, but I didn't need to see those items to know he was a cowhand of the Texas persuasion. He stumped my way with a stiff-legged limp, and I figured he'd turned saddle maker after one too many horse wrecks.

"Howdy," he said. "Somethin' ah can do for y'all?"

I fished the spur rowel I'd found at the cottonwood grove out of my vest pocket. "Howdy," I said. "I'm lookin' for a rowel like this one."

He took the rowel from me and studied it awhile. Then he handed it back. "Don't see many six-pointed star rowels," he said. "Might be special made. It yours?"

"I guess it is now," I said, smiling. "Found it this mornin' over near Sage Creek."

The saddler was silent for a moment, studying me through narrowed eyes. "Only man I know in these parts who wears a six-pointed star rowel," he said, "is Ross Devlin, owner of the Rafter D. You know Ross?"

"We've met," I said.

Fifteen

BEARER OF BAD NEWS

Out on the street again, I gave some thought to the saddle maker's words. *"Only man I know in these parts who wears a six-pointed star rowel is Ross Devlin, from the Rafter D."*

On the one hand, I was not surprised. Devlin had made his feelings crystal clear from the first day I met him—rustling in the Big Open had to be stopped, no matter what it took to do it. On the other hand, Devlin made an effort to distance himself from the activities of the men who called themselves regulators. They were working in a good cause, he implied, but that didn't mean he approved or authorized their methods. He had made himself scarce the day his boys roughed me up, for instance. Nobody could blame *him* if his regulators got a mite out of hand.

If the rowel I'd found at the cottonwood grove belonged to Devlin, that would indicate he not only took part in Irv Baker's lynching but likely ordered it as well. In the end it all boiled down to this: I *knew* Devlin was behind the rustler clean-up but I still couldn't *prove* it. And even if I could have, most folks in the Big Open would consider him more hero than villain. I

might have felt that way myself if I hadn't been Chance Ridgeway's deputy as long as I had. To Ridgeway, the law was the *law,* with no shades of grey. If it wasn't written down in a law book somewhere, the end *never* justified the means.

I was not as hard-nosed as Ridgeway. I believed the law was mostly right but sometimes wrong, and that what is lawful is not always what is just. I did not believe Irv Baker was a cow thief, but Ross's regulators had hung him for one. Stringing up an innocent man was not only unpleasant for the man himself, but also for his wife and kids.

I went back inside the saddle shop. "Say, pardner," I said. "Does this town have a public telephone?"

"Over at the hotel," the saddler said. "Ask the desk clerk."

The desk clerk at the Treasure State was busy playing solitaire when I came in, and he didn't look up from his game when I approached his desk. "Red six on the black seven," I said. "Can I ask you a question?"

The clerk made a face like I had interrupted the reading of his rich uncle's will. He looked me over and elected to be unimpressed. "Sure, cowboy," said he. "You want to reserve the Presidential Suite?"

"Not today," I said, "but I would like to make a telephone call. To Miles City."

The desk clerk played a black ten on a black jack. "Telephone call will cost you a dollar, bub. Have you *got* a dollar?"

"Sure have," I said, and laid a cartwheel on the desk blotter.

The clerk sighed and pushed back from the desk. Pointing to an alcove near the front door, he said, "Telephone is on the wall yonder. Turn the crank and talk to the operator."

"I'll do that," said I. "When I get through with my call I might even show you how to play that game. The way you're goin', you're liable to need a bigger deck."

When my call to the Sheriff's office at Miles City went through, it was not Tom Irvine who answered, but one of his deputies. "Tom is over in Bozeman, testifyin' at a trial," the deputy said. "He won't be back 'til Tuesday week."

I faltered for a moment. Memories of the shooting at the bank returned with the mention of Tom Irvine's name. In spite of all I'd done to put my life as a lawman behind me, circumstance was drawing me back. Static hummed and whined on the line like wind through the sagebrush. It was a lonesome sound.

"My name's Merlin Fanshaw," I said. "Tell Tom I called. I'm ridin' for the C Heart outfit east of Fairfax. There's been some trouble here."

"I'll tell him," the deputy said. "What sort of trouble?"

"Cow men hereabouts are huntin' rustlers," I said. "They just strung up an innocent man."

"You know that for a fact?"

"It's what I believe," I said, knowing how weak that must sound.

"This feller they strung up. What was his name?"

"Irv Baker. Homesteader from over on Sage Creek."

"I'll tell Tom you called," the deputy said. "So long."

As I passed the desk on my way out, the clerk lifted his eyes from his cards. He said, "I thought you were going to show me how to play this game."

I shook my head. "Changed my mind," I said. "A man has to play his own hand, whether he's dealin' solitaire or just livin' his life."

Alex was sitting under an apple tree outside the funeral parlor when I came back. He got to his feet when he saw me ride up and met me with a shy smile. He looked lonesome and lost, and it caused me to recall the way I felt seven years before when I lost my own Pa. I was eighteen then, older than Alex by two years, but I remembered the hurt as if it was yesterday.

I drew rein and smiled. "All through here?"

Alex nodded. "Yes, sir. Mr. Grimsrud says he'll keep my pa on ice until Ma and the young'uns

can come in for the buryin'. He said not to wait too long."

"All right. Mount up."

Alex swung up onto the roan and turned away toward the road back to the ranch. "I'm ready," he said. "Like you say when we're workin' back at the C Heart, 'we're burnin' daylight.' "

Yes, I thought. *And we're meltin' ice.*

Twilight had come to the home ranch by the time we rode in. The stubborn skies clung to the last traces of daylight, but already a few stars had appeared. At the main house lamplight burned yellow in the windows, and I felt rather than saw that people waited in the darkness. Drawing rein at the gate, I made out Billie's slender form.

"Evening, Merlin . . . Alex," she said. "Everything all right with you boys?"

"Yes," I said. I couldn't bring myself to say "body" or "corpse" in front of Alex. "We took Mr. Baker into Fairfax. He's at the funeral parlor there."

Billie's voice was tender. "Alex," she said. "You must be starved. There's antelope stew on the stove and biscuits in the oven."

"Thank you, ma'am," Alex said, "but I . . . I ain't all that hungry this evenin'."

"Of course you are," Billie said. "You're sixteen. Try and eat a bite or two—you wouldn't want to hurt Maggie's feelings, would you?"

I heard leather creak in the darkness as Alex dismounted. "No, ma'am. I wouldn't want that," he said. I heard the scuff of his boots on the plank walkway, and then the opening of the front door.

I stepped down, too. All at once I was bone tired and wolf hungry myself. Behind Billie in the darkness, I caught the glint of metal. "Antelope stew, huh? Who shot the antelope?"

Clem Guthrie lowered the Winchester. "I did," he said. "With this here rifle. Who did you think?"

"It's a little dark to still be huntin' now, isn't it?"

"We heard horses," Clem said. "Didn't know for sure it was you."

"It's me," I said.

I turned to Billie. "I told that city marshal, Bentwood, about the fire and the lynching. He wasn't all that interested. Said it was outside his jurisdiction. Seemed glad it was."

Clem exploded. "Bentwood!" he snorted. "That dough-bellied coward wouldn't make a pimple on a peace officer's arse!"

Catching himself, Clem mumbled, "Um . . . *sorry,* Billie."

"Crudely put, but accurate," Billie said. "What then, Merlin?"

"We took the body over to the funeral parlor on River Street, and I left Alex with Grimsrud, the undertaker. I went down to the hotel and

telephoned Tom Irvine over at Miles City. Tom was away on business, but I made my report to his deputy.

"One thing more. I lined up a funeral for Irv. Told Grimsrud we'd let him know when."

"Irv Baker's poor wife," Billie said. "And the children. Burned out of their home, and poor as church mice. I'll pay for the funeral, of course."

My eyes were growing accustomed to the darkness. Billie turned into the light from the windows and I saw tears in her eyes. "The family is staying in the bunkhouse. Clem rigged up bunks for you and him in the barn."

"Sorry to be the bearer of so much bad news, Billie," I said.

Shining in the lamplight, Billie's eyes met mine. "You did well," she said. "I've come to depend on you, more than you know."

I dropped my eyes, abashed and discomfited by her gaze. "You *can,*" I said.

Sixteen

MAGGIE TAKES OFFENSE

It sure beat all how fast word traveled in the Big Open. In a land where settlers were few and a man's nearest neighbor might be ten miles distant, news seemed to spread with the speed of light.

That's how it was with the lynching of Irv Baker and the burning of his house. Almost as soon as those dire events occurred, cow men, sheep ranchers, and homesteaders all across the area seemed to know about them. From as far away as the Yellowstone and the Tongue, folks came to inquire after the Baker family and to offer their help.

The day we held Irv's funeral was sunny and windy, with clouds moving across the sky like ships under sail. Maybe forty people attended, most of them homesteaders like the Bakers, but only a few had known the family. Folks came to give such comfort as they could, uneasy with the knowledge that what happened to Irv might very well happen to them.

The local gospel sharp from the Methodist church had not known the family either, but he read from the scriptures and offered such

consolation as might be had. Martha Baker sat in a chair from the mortuary in a black dress and veil, with her children gathered close about her. A sudden gust of wind rattled grit against the pine box that held Irv's remains and left a speck of dust in my eye. My eye commenced to water, of course, but I have to confess it wasn't entirely on account of the speck.

Afterward, we lowered the coffin into Irv's grave and his sons Jake and Alex shoveled loose dirt atop it until the hole was filled. I told the preacher much obliged on behalf of the family and offered him a modest stipend. Maybe it wasn't as modest as I thought because he gave me a big smile and told me he'd pray for me.

Billie settled up with the undertaker and we all told Martha how sorry we were for her trouble. Then Clem drove her and the children back to their place on Sage Creek, where her neighbors were already making plans to help rebuild her house.

Now you would think the kindness of strangers and the send-off at the cemetery might have taken away some of the hurt from Irv's untimely death, and maybe for Martha and the kids it did. But a dark wind was blowing through the Big Open, and in that land where law was scarce, night riders were filling the gap with a rough justice of their own. I recalled Irv's face the day we cut his body down, and the grief his hanging

caused his family. I remembered my old boss, Chance Ridgeway, who believed no man had a right to be neutral in the presence of evil, but should—and in his opinion, *must*—take a firm stand against it.

I was a lawman no longer, but a cowhand for the C Heart. And yet, like Ridgeway, I still saw things in terms of good and evil, right and wrong. Ridgeway could never turn his back on what he believed was right. Neither, it seemed, could I.

With the return of Martha Baker and her brood to their farm, the C Heart seemed quiet, even a mite lonesome. Billie rode out most days to check on her cows and calves. Clem and me moved back into the bunkhouse and got ready to start putting up hay. And Maggie took care of the house and cooked for the outfit. We didn't talk much about the night riders, but that doesn't mean they weren't on our minds. Hardly a day passed that one or another of us didn't search the nearby hills for signs of horsemen on the move, or perk up at what seemed to be the sound of hoofbeats. Clem took to wearing a pistol even while he rode the mowing machine. Billie carried a Winchester in her saddle scabbard whenever she rode out away from the ranch. And Maggie kept a loaded twelve-gauge propped up in a corner of the kitchen.

As for me, I was cleaning out the stalls in the

barn on a quiet afternoon when I heard the clatter of hoofbeats on the bridge. I still refused to carry a firearm on my person, believing that if I did not pack a pistol I would not soon again slay a child, but my heart did a quick-step when I heard the rider coming, and for a moment I regretted my prudence.

Walking out of the dark barn into sunlight, it was a moment before I recognized Ross Devlin, coming fast on a lathered thoroughbred up to the main house. I met him just as he reached the gate. He pulled back hard on the reins, bringing his horse to a sliding stop and stepping down onto the roadway.

His handsome face was a bitter mask. He scowled, his eyes flashing. When he spoke, his voice was tight as rawhide. "Fanshaw," he said.

"Hello, Ross," I said. "I was about to ask you to step down, but I see you already have."

"I've no time to stand on ceremony," he said. "I'm here to see Billie. Go get her."

I didn't care much for his attitude. I felt my face grow hot. The taste of bile rose at the back of my throat. When I replied, my voice didn't sound like my own. "I don't believe I will," I said. "I expect Billie already knows you're here. If she wants to see you, she'll come out. If she doesn't, you can get the hell off the place just as fast as you came in."

Ross's face flushed beet red. "You cocky little

bastard," he said. "You're just a damned hired hand. You don't own this outfit."

I gave him a cold smile. "Neither do *you,* Devlin. Not yet."

Behind me, the screen door opened and closed. Then Billie's voice: "Step aside, Merlin," she said. "I'll speak to Ross."

I turned. Billie stood on the walkway behind me, dignity in every line of her. She was dressed in her riding clothes, and her well-worn Stetson was pulled level just above her eyes. She looked up at Devlin and smiled. "All right," she said. "What is it?"

Devlin's face changed. Meeting Billie's eyes, he had enough presence of mind to doff his hat. "I . . . That is, we . . . I'm afraid I have bad news," he said.

Billie's expression didn't change. Waiting, she thanked me with her eyes. I walked away, toward the gate. Billie turned back to Devlin.

"It's the bank," Devlin said. "E.B. has cancelled your loan extension. He's calling in your note after all."

Devlin showed her the palms of his hands. "I argued on your behalf," he said, "but E.B. has to answer to his depositors. He says he's sorry, but there's nothing he can do."

"Oh," Billie said. "I don't think that's exactly true. How much time do I have?"

"Two weeks."

For the first time, I saw Billie falter. There was a hesitation, a quiver in her voice. "Oh," she said. "That really isn't much time."

"You don't have to lose this place," Devlin said. "I told you I'll take care of you. You can keep your ranch and share all I have besides."

Billie shook her head. When she spoke her voice was controlled and firm, "No," she said. "I really can't do that. I don't love you, Ross."

Devlin grasped Billie's upper arms with both hands. "You little fool!" he said. "Don't you know what I can *give* you?"

Billie struggled against Devlin's grip. I took a long stride toward them, and heard the screen door bang again. Maggie was outside, clad in her house dress and apron. The shotgun was in her hands, held high and pointed at Ross Devlin.

"Take your hands off her, you lecherous cur!" Maggie said. "Haven't you caused this family *enough* misery?"

Surprised, Devlin stared wide-eyed at Maggie and the twelve-gauge. Abruptly, he released his grip on Billie's arms and stepped back. Billie stumbled, falling to one knee beside the walkway.

Maggie's voice trembled with rage. She cocked both hammers on the shotgun and took aim at Devlin's chest. "Get on your horse and off this place, you damned skunk! *Get!*"

Devlin's face was ashen. He took a step

backward, one hand extended toward Maggie. "Be careful, Margaret," he said. "You don't know what a gun like that can do!"

"The hell I don't," Maggie replied. "Get mounted and gone, or I'll kill you dead as yesterday's hash!"

Devlin took another two steps back, away from Maggie's fury, and then turned and caught up the reins of the thoroughbred. In another moment he was mounted and staring at Maggie, Billie, and me.

"All right," he said. "I can protect you no longer—now you'll face the consequences of your stupid pride!"

"It's coming," he said. "Mark my words. *A fire storm is coming!*"

Maggie pointed the shotgun at the sky and touched off a shot. The thoroughbred bolted, nearly unseating Devlin, and then raced with its rider back over the bridge and away from the C Heart.

Billie was back on her feet. She stood staring at Maggie as if she'd never seen her before. Maggie lowered both the shotgun and her eyes. Thinking I'd lighten the moment a bit, I joshed Maggie some. "Boy howdy!" I said. "Now I *know* I don't want to get on your bad side!"

Maggie wasn't listening. She stood, her eyes downcast, avoiding Billie's eyes. "Maggie," Billie said. "You asked Ross if he hadn't caused

my family enough misery. *How* did Ross Devlin cause my family misery?"

"I . . . I don't know. When he put his hands on you I just got mad. I didn't know what I was saying."

Billie took the shotgun from Maggie and placed her arm about her friend. "It was sweet of you to come to my defense," Billie said, "but threatening to shoot Ross just might have been a little over the top. Don't you think?"

Maggie shook her head. "No," she said. "I meant what I said. I'd have killed that toplofty bastard. I really *would* have."

I didn't know about Billie, but I'd seen the expression on Maggie's face when she threw down on Devlin with the twelve-gauge. *I* believed her.

That evening Billie held a war council up at the main house. We four—Billie, Maggie, Clem, and me—took our places around the dinner table and waited for Billie to open the ball. "I'm in a tight place," she said, "but we're not whipped until we quit. I'm not inclined to quit.

"In the morning," she continued, "I'll take the wagon into Fairfax and pick up enough groceries to see us through for awhile. If we're in for a siege, or a fight with night riders, we'll need food and supplies."

Clem studied the contents of his coffee cup and scowled. "We'll need cartridges for the rifles and

pistols. And shells for Maggie's twelve-gauge, in case she decides to run off another beef baron."

Maggie squinted at Clem and raised an eyebrow. "I wouldn't get too lippy if I were you," she said. "I cook for this outfit, but I also put out poison for the rats. It'd be a shame if I got my duties mixed."

Clem's eyes shone in the light of the oil lamp on the table, the way they did when he was pleased but not inclined to show it. Maggie held her hard look as long as she could, and then broke it with a quick smile. I was reminded how much these people cared about each other, and in that moment realized they had made me a full member of their clan.

"What about your note at the bank?" I asked. "Two weeks doesn't give you much time."

Billie sipped her coffee. "There's a cattle buyer in Miles City," she said. "I think I might be able to contract my calves with him. Maybe the cows, too. That would make the C Heart a ranch without cattle, but it might save the place."

I nodded. "You could always take in cattle on shares until you can afford to restock," I said. "The C Heart has good grass and water—and the 'soup kitchen' besides."

Billie smiled. "Yes," she said. "Maybe I could do that."

Her smile faded. For a moment Billie was silent, studying the coffee in her cup. Then she

raised her eyes, looking at the three of us in turn. "What about Ross?" she asked. "Do you think he really means to cause us trouble?"

Clem rose halfway out of his chair. "Hell *yes* he does! Ross Devlin's regulators already hung Merlin from a damn tree! Beside that, I believe him and that scum-suckin' banker are in cahoots! Ross Devlin is after your ranch, girl—any way he can get it!"

Sadness touched Billie's face and faded. She smiled a wistful smile. "Don't be shy, Clem," she said. "Tell us what you *really* think.

"All right," she said. "Clem and I will take the wagon into Fairfax and pick up the things we need. I'll telephone the cattle buyer while I'm there. Merlin and Maggie can stay here and hold down the fort."

Clem stood up. "Then I guess I'd best go ask Jack and Jill if they want to go to town. If they say 'yes' I'll hitch 'em to the wagon."

"If they say 'no' hitch 'em up anyway," Billie said. "You don't want to have to pull that wagon all the way to Fairfax by yourself, do you?"

Seventeen

BECKY'S STORY

Next morning, I helped Clem hitch the work team to the wagon. He was looking forward to the trip to town, and I knew he was hoping he'd have time for a trip to the saloon while he was waiting on Billie. He adjusted the throat latch on Jill's bridle and squinted against the sun. "What are you fixin' to do while we're gone?" he asked.

"I'm still a little stiff from my hangin' and from the dust-up with Sam Bodie," I said. "Thought I'd split some kindling for Maggie's cook stove and work some of the kinks out."

"Good idea. If we get to fightin' night riders and such, we won't have much time to tend the chores."

I made no answer, but Clem didn't let that stop the conversation. "I saw that gun and holster you keep in your bedroll," he said. "Good-lookin' firearm. Forty-five, is it?"

"No. Forty-four. It's a gun with a history."

"Ain't they all?"

Clem rubbed his beard stubble and gave me his one-eyed squint. "I know you have some kind of religious *scruple* or somethin' about packin' a hand gun," he said, "but say you back-slid or somethin' and changed your mind. Do

you reckon you could use a gun if you had to?"

I grinned. "You reckon you could ask a longer and more complicated question? Yeah, I guess I could use a six-gun if push came to shove."

"Well, it occurs to me push just might come to shove if we find ourselves hip deep in night riders and regulators some evenin'. I guess what I'm askin' is, how many cartridges do you have for that smoke pole? I mean I *could* fetch you some from town."

"I suppose I have about forty. That would take care of two score of regulators, maybe more if I get two with one shot. But I guess I *would* be in trouble if forty-one showed up. You'd better bring me a box or two."

"Just thought I'd ask. I didn't know . . . I thought you might be too bashful to shoot night riders or somethin'. I have *two* pistols myself, a cap and ball Colt's Army and my old forty-five. Got a thirty-two around here somewheres, but it ain't worth a damn."

Clem could always make me laugh. "Go on ahead, Wild Bill. Pick up the boss lady and go to town. I'll *watch* you shoot sometime if I can find a safe place to stand."

"Anywhere behind me, Merlin," he said.

I watched as Clem and Billie headed out for Fairfax, and then I walked over behind the house and took a look at the wood pile. Short sections of

dry cottonwood and ash were stacked in rows against the house, and a four-pound axe stood imbedded in a chopping block. I pulled the axe free and placed a chunk on the block. Then I took a good stance and went to work.

I was still working thirty minutes later, busting chunks with a rhythm and a will. I found I had split a decent supply of stove wood and that I'd also worked up an appetite. I sank the axe blade into the chopping block and commenced to stack the kindling.

"Good job, cowboy."

I looked up to see Maggie watching me from the corner of the house. She was dressed as she had been the first time I saw her, in a man's sheepskin coat and her house dress and apron. Maggie shaded her eyes with her hand and smiled. "Bring an armload of that wood and come inside," she said. "I've made a fresh batch of bear sign."

"Bear sign?"

"Sure. You know—doughnuts. I thought maybe a hard-workin' range rider like yourself could eat a few."

"You came to the right man, Maggie Adair. I never met a doughnut I didn't like."

"Well, come on, then," she said. "They aren't going to eat themselves."

The kitchen was warm after the cool air of the morning outside. I took a seat at the table and

Maggie set a blue china plate containing a half-dozen fresh doughnuts before me. Then she poured me a cup of coffee and sat down across from me. I recalled that I had thought Maggie a homely woman when first we met, and I marveled at the changes a few weeks can bring. Five minutes in Maggie's company and a man forgot the deep wrinkles and sun-browned skin of her face, remembering instead her honest spirit and the quiet good humor in her smile.

Maggie took the makings from the pocket of her sheepskin and tapped tobacco onto a cigarette paper. Tightening the sack's drawstring with her teeth, she smoothed out the tobacco and shaped the paper into a cylinder. Then she licked the paper, twisted the end, and placed the quirly in her mouth. Popping a match to flame with her thumb-nail, she lit the cigarette and drew smoke deep into her lungs. Pushing the sack toward me, she raised her eyebrows. "Smoke?" she asked.

I shook my head. "I don't use tobacco," I replied, "I neither smoke nor chew." Taking a bite of doughnut, I said, "Bear sign, pie and such are *my* weaknesses."

Maggie looked at her cigarette as if she'd never seen one before. "I'd be better off if *I* didn't use it," she said. "But like the man said, my virtues are written in sand and my vices are carved in stone."

"I wouldn't know about your vices," I said. "All I've seen so far are your virtues."

"Name one."

"Well, first off, you're a beautiful woman."

"*Beautiful?* Hell, cowboy, you need somebody to check your eyesight! The *last* thing I am is *pretty*."

"Never said *pretty*. Said *beautiful*. Pretty is gold *plate,* beautiful is solid *gold*."

"Never trust a silver-tongued cowboy," she said. "What about my other virtues?"

"I'll name four. You're a fine cook. You're hard-working. You have a pleasant disposition. And you're loyal to your friends."

Maggie laughed. "I'm not so sure about the pleasant disposition," she said. "I can be a hot-tempered, double-rectified *harridan* sometimes."

I smiled. "You mean like when you run cattle kings off the place at gunpoint? I guess I'd call *that* bein' loyal to a friend."

Maggie made no answer. I took a sip of coffee. I heard the stove ping. For a long moment neither of us spoke.

Then Maggie broke the silence. "I guess you're wondering why I came on so strong yesterday."

I nodded. "You asked him, 'Haven't you caused this family *enough* misery?' Sounds like you and Devlin have an old score to settle. Something even Billie doesn't know about."

Maggie took a deep puff on her cigarette and exhaled blue smoke. "Something *nobody* knows but me," she said. "Something Billie must *never* know. It would break her heart."

She stood, and walked to the stove. Lifting the stove lid, she took a last drag on her cigarette and dropped it into the flames. Then she turned. "I've carried the secret alone for too long," she said. "I need to share it with someone. Someone I can trust. Maybe I need to share it with *you*."

Maggie's honest brown eyes searched mine. All at once, I felt uneasy. Maybe, I thought, what she wanted to tell me was something I shouldn't hear. I wanted to say her secret was none of my business. I feared the cost of knowing, and I wanted to walk away from the trust I saw in her eyes.

In the end, I tried to have it both ways. "Well," I said. "You can *trust* me with your secret, but I'm not sure I'm the one you should be tellin'. I mean I'm surely not a priest, nor a father confessor, neither."

She smiled. "Hush. Are you going to let me tell you or not?"

I swallowed half a cup of coffee in one gulp. "Let 'er rip," I said.

Maggie filled our cups and put the pot back on the stove. Then she sat down again across from me and began to speak.

"Billie's mother—Rebecca—was my friend," she said. "Except no one ever called her Rebecca; most people called her 'Becky'. Well, Becky was a city girl from the east, out to see the west. She met Calvin, Billie's father, on a horse ranch west

of Miles City owned by Duncan Thompson, a remittance man from Edinburgh. Calvin worked for Duncan but he had ambitions of his own—Calvin wanted his own ranch and his own cattle. The day he met Becky, he came up with *another* ambition—to make Becky his wife and the mother of his children.

"And that's how it turned out. Calvin swept Becky off her feet and on to her new role as a cattleman's wife. Duncan helped the young couple finance their dream—this ranch, and the beginnings of their own herd.

"Calvin and Becky were great favorites with their neighbors, although this country was sparsely settled then and neighbors were few and far between. They still are. My dad had a small place north of here, and Becky and I became fast friends. Calvin built this house for her and brought in Durham cattle. He loved the solitude and the wild open country. Becky was pleased for her husband, but unhappy. In her heart, she longed for civilization, and the social life she left behind her back east.

"Billie was born during the winter of their first year here, and for a time Becky was happy just raising her pretty young daughter. Calvin doted on the child, and Billie adored her dad. He taught her to ride when she was scarcely more than a toddler, and he took her with him everywhere. Billie said once, 'I was the son he never had.'

"Meanwhile, Becky seemed to grow more unhappy with each year. I visited when I could, and some of the other families made a point of stopping by, but the bright, pretty woman I remembered from the first days of our friendship seemed to be slipping away, pulling into some lonely place inside herself.

"Like Becky, I married young. My husband was a wild young horseman and trader who lived for adventure. In the second year of our marriage, he was killed by a Cheyenne war party in a dispute over some horses. I never considered marrying again; I couldn't imagine loving another man the way I'd loved my husband, and I wasn't willing to settle for less.

"I spent more and more time with Becky, and with Billie. I suppose in a way, they became my family.

"Becky became more withdrawn. More and more, I took over Billie's care. I taught her to read and do her sums. I shared what I knew of sewing and cooking. Billie was bright and a quick learner, whatever the subject, but she missed a mother's warmth. I walked a narrow line, trying not to compete for her affection but giving her the love her mother could not, or would not, provide.

"When Billie grew older, Calvin and Becky sent her back east to boarding school, and they found themselves alone together in a home that once was happy but had become a sort of prison.

As Becky became more withdrawn, Calvin found escape in the new town of Fairfax. He began to drink heavily and gamble—anyone will tell you *that's* a bad combination—and he found common ground with the chippies and barflies who shared his interests, and his money."

Maggie paused, remembering. Getting up from the table, she walked over to the stove. Lifting the lid, she added two new fresh lengths of split ash from the wood box to the coals and replaced the lids. I heard the wood catch fire, heard the stove hum and ping as the metal expanded. Maggie brought the coffee pot to the table and poured a warm-up to our cups. Then she sat down again.

"Then one day Ross Devlin stopped by the house. He said he was looking for Calvin, but the truth is he knew perfectly well where Calvin was. He was really looking for Becky.

"I guess what happened next wasn't all that surprising. Becky was lonely, longing for a gentler world of mannered men and charming ladies. Ross was handsome and a ladies man who knew how to say what a lonely woman wanted to hear. They began a love affair that mostly involved Ross coming by for an hour or two whenever Calvin wasn't home. Since Calvin's life was mostly spent at the faro tables and saloons of Fairfax, Becky and Ross had plenty of chances to carry on their trysts."

Maggie frowned. "Well, it wasn't long before

Calvin found himself in financial trouble. He couldn't afford to keep Billie in boarding school any longer, which was all right with her. She loved life on the ranch and wanted nothing more than to come back to it. Billie came home.

"As Becky's best—maybe her only—real friend, I knew about her and Ross. Becky told me herself, and made me promise to keep her secret. I did everything I could think of to get her to break it off with Ross; I knew his reputation and saw nothing but hurt ahead for my friend. But Becky wouldn't listen. She was convinced that Ross Devlin was the love of her life. The truth is he was more like an addiction to opium or whiskey—something she had to have even though it was destroying her.

"Billie spent much of her time with me. Somehow, I kept her from finding out about Becky and Ross. She took an interest in the ranch and in working with the cattle, and she helped pick up the slack her dad had left.

"In the end, Ross grew tired of Becky and broke off the affair. Someone new—someone younger—came along, I suppose."

"What happened then?"

"Becky couldn't accept the breakup. She ran after Ross, made a public spectacle of herself. Wouldn't let him alone. He held firm, finally offered her cash to stay out of his life. You can imagine how Becky took that. She'd given

herself completely to Ross, abandoning her husband and even her daughter. And when she finally surrenders the last shred of her pride, what does Ross do? He offers her *money*, like a john paying a whore."

Maggie wept then, tears flowing freely. "The heartless bastard tossed her away like an empty wine bottle. Becky left Montana, and moved into a boarding house in Bismarck. Two weeks later the landlady found her dead in the bathtub. Becky had slit her wrists with a razor."

For a long time Maggie said nothing. She walked over to the front windows and stood staring out toward the distant mountains. Her back was turned toward me, and when she spoke again her voice was so soft I could hardly make out her words.

"Neither Calvin nor Billie ever knew about Becky's romance with Ross. They—and most of the people in town—thought she had a mental breakdown, that the lonesome life of a rancher's wife was just too much for her. I guess, in a way, it was.

"Calvin grieved her in his way; I always thought he blamed himself for her death. And then he died, too. Killed in a horse wreck late one night as he was heading back to the ranch."

"And everything fell on Billie," I said.

"Yes," Maggie said. "Her mother's suicide, her father's death, and the debts he'd incurred. Billie

was determined to pay off the note at the bank and get the C Heart on a paying basis. I admired her for that.

"But then, as if she didn't have *enough* to deal with, who should come sniffing around her door? *Ross Devlin!* The miserable wretch who drove her mother to her *grave!*"

Eighteen
PREPARING FOR VISITORS

When Maggie finished her story of Billie's folks—and of Ross Devlin's part in the whole sorry affair—she slumped back with a sigh. She closed her eyes. Her hands lay relaxed in her lap. It was as if she had carried a heavy burden too long, and now having shared its weight she could rest for a spell.

As for me, I was of two minds. On the one hand, I was glad Maggie figured she could trust me with her secret. On the other hand, now that I knew it, my life was a good deal more complicated.

I said as much. "I'm pleased that you trusted me enough to share your story," I said. "But I have to admit I was happier before I knew.

"Puts me in mind of a story they say Honest Abe once told. Seems folks in this small village were fixin' to run a jackleg gambler out of their town on a rail. They asked the gambler how he felt about that, and he replied, 'Well, it's all right, I suppose . . . but if it wasn't for the *honor* of the thing, I'd just as soon *walk*.'"

Maggie's laugh was full-bodied and straight from the belly. "Sorry, cowboy," she said. "You

were ridin' for Billie, but now you're part of the family. You know what they say about eggs and bacon. It's a meal where the *chicken* is *involved,* but the *pig* is *committed.*"

I joined in her laughter. "Who are you callin' a *pig?*" I said.

Clem and Billie came home just before sundown. Watching from a vantage point on the low hill above the main house, I heard the wagon's clatter as it rounded the bend and began its final pull up the lane. More and more now, especially since the raid on the Baker place, my mind was on the night riders.

I was surprised to find I'd been holding my breath. When first I heard the hoofbeats of the team on the road, I went tense as stretched wire and my heartbeat went from a walk to a gallop. Seeing Clem at the reins of the work team and Billie beside him, I breathed easy and walked down to meet them.

Billie smiled at my approach. Clem's gap-toothed grin was just a little too wide. *Son of a gun has had more than a beer or two,* I thought.

Clem was in a happy mood. "You're just in time to help haul the grub into the house," he said. "I'm not feelin' all that steady on my feet."

I gave Billie a hand down. "Appears you let the cat get into the catnip," I said.

Billie shook her head. "Old tomcats are hard to

control," she said. "By the time I finished shopping, it was all Clem could do to find the wagon, let alone load it."

"Always go shoppin' with a woman," Clem said. "A man can get downright mellow by the time she's through buyin' fooforaw and fumadiddle."

Catching Billie's eye, I asked, "Any trouble?"

"No," she said. "Some of those Texas men were in town. And the man they call Maddox. They stood outside the livery barn and watched us go past, but that's all they did—just watched."

Clem wasn't quite as unsteady as he appeared. He lifted a crate of groceries from the wagon bed and staggered toward the house with it. "Them *pistoleros* ain't so tough," he said. "When they seen I was wearin' my forty-five, they sure pulled in their horns."

I watched Clem amble away with the crate. Sure enough, he wore his holstered six-shooter on his right hip. I felt a sudden chill deep in my belly. Turning to Billie, I said. "That's the last time Clem wears his gun in town," I said. "We can't let it happen again!"

Billie gave me a sharp look. She opened her mouth to reply, and then I saw her eyes widen in sudden understanding.

"Oh!" she said. "I . . . I didn't think. . . ."

I touched her sleeve. "I didn't mean to startle you," I said. "It's just that sometimes a town dog will *hurt* an old tomcat."

I lay awake for a long time that night, listening to Clem's soft snoring and the patter of raindrops on the bunkhouse roof. The rain meant there would be no work for Clem and me in the hayfields the next day and that such hay as was already down would have to be turned and dried before we could stack. Even with Billie's growing troubles and the threats we faced, I could not seem to round up my thoughts and get them corralled.

How could I have known even a month before how close I would become to the people at the C Heart? The caring between us had grown in small ways, a smile here, and a shared hardship there, until of late I found that Billie, Maggie, and Clem were the nearest thing to kinfolk I'd known since my pa died.

Billie had shown her trust in me by word and by deed of. Maggie had shared her terrible secret after years of bearing its burden alone. And Clem—foolish, goodhearted, loyal Clem—had liked me from the start. A man of quick temper and hard judgments, Clem now relied on me more and more for assurance and direction.

I smiled. In his bunk across the room, Clem tossed and turned in his blankets, his leg moving like a sleeping hound's in a dream of rabbits. What were Clem's dreams, I wondered. Did he dash across some remembered meadow as a boy? Did he lope up a mountainside as a hunter

chasing elk? Or maybe he merely leaned on the polished bar at the Mint Saloon, trying to hook his boot heel over the rail.

Cold fear had clutched my heart when I heard his boast: *Them pistoleros ain't so tough. When they seen I was wearin' my forty-five they sure pulled in their horns.*

Clearly, Clem had no idea of the true nature of gun hands. Men like Maddox and his so-called regulators were as far beyond the ordinary citizen in the shootist's deadly art as fire is from ice. Clem might as well have said: *Them rattlesnakes ain't so deadly. They sure backed off when they seen I was wearin' shoes.*

As a kid growing up I fooled around with all manner of firearms, but it was not until the summer of '84 when Garrett Sinclair gave me his "short course on the art of deadly force" that I began to understand what gun fighting was all about. Garrett ran a livery barn in Maiden, Montana then, but as a young man he'd served as a peace officer in Kansas under Hickok at Abilene and had worked Dodge City with the Mastersons.

I can hear him now. "Get the idea of fair play out of your mind altogether," he said. "Killin' ain't a game. When you go up against a man who's tryin' to snuff your candle, only one thing matters—that you live and he don't."

"Go into the fight with every advantage you can

muster," he said. "Go in with your gun drawn, with the sun at your back and in the other man's eyes. Charge him from on horseback, ambush him from behind a tree, shoot him in the back, the belly, or wherever. Shoot him 'til he's down, then keep on a-shootin' 'til he's dead. Never forget he'll be tryin' his damnedest to do the same to you."

Garrett brought it down to basics. "Practice until your gun handling is second nature," he'd said. "Take your time and make the first shot count. Speed is fine, but accuracy is forever. Go into the fight with no hesitation at all. Most men will balk at taking another man's life. For a split second they'll pause. The true gun fighter will not, and if *you* do you may well be dead."

I feared for Clem Guthrie's life not because he *didn't* carry a gun, but because he *did*. One of the oldest tricks in the gunman's book was pushing an unskilled and untaught victim into reaching for a weapon. The gun fighter could then kill him in "self defense" which was, in truth, plain murder.

Yes, I thought, I remember your teaching, Garrett, but what you *didn't* tell me is that a man can do all you taught and still wind up killing an unarmed boy in the shadows of a cow town bank. Hard men might soon be coming to the C Heart. How could Billie, Maggie, and Clem stand against them unless I took a hand? More and

more, they looked to me as their leader. It seemed to me they might have made a better choice.

My fingers reached beneath the soogans of my bedroll and touched the ivory grips of my forty-four. *It's a gun with a history,* I told Clem, and it was all of that. A legacy from my friend Orville Mooney, the revolver was well-balanced and sweet-shooting. Orville had pulled it too slow against a horse thief and had cashed in his checks on the streets of Shenanigan, Montana. I had packed it ever since.

The weapon had seen service against kidnappers in the Pryor Mountains, in the killing of a murderer in the Big Horns, and in a shoot-out in the depths of a Butte copper mine. Yes, and in the killing of Toby Slocum at the State National Bank. Could I take it up again, even to defend my friends? I honestly didn't know.

At the bunkhouse, I took my holstered gun from my bedroll and strapped it on. As I settled the weapon's weight in its remembered place at my right hip, I found I was holding my breath. I stood tall, exhaled, and walked out into the sunshine.

When Clem saw me wearing the Colt his bloodshot eyes went wide as saucers. "Well, I declare!" he said. "You're packin' a six-gun!"

"You have a real gift for pointin' out the obvious," I said. "Thought I'd do a little target practice over behind the barn. See if I can still operate this old black-eyed Susan."

"Wait for me," Clem said. "I'll fetch my forty-five and come with you!"

"Bring a few cans and bottles," I said. "I'll stop by the house and let the women know what we're up to. Let 'em know we're not 'regulators' payin' a call."

I found Maggie outside, hanging wet wash on the clothesline. Her glance was quick, and it lingered on my waist. "You're all dressed up," she said.

Seemed like *everyone* was stating the obvious. "Yeah," I said. "I noticed that."

"I'll be doin' a little pistol practice with Clem this mornin'," I said. "Didn't want you and Billie to worry if you hear shootin'."

Maggie pinned a dish towel to the line. "Thanks for the notice, cowboy," she said. "In case you gun down that old coot by mistake, let me know. I'll set one less place for dinner."

Clem was waiting out back of the barn. His holstered forty-five was on his hip, and he held a gunny sack in his right hand. "Gathered up some targets," he said. "Couldn't come up with many tin cans, but I found plenty of bottles."

"Imagine that," I said. "I expect you knew most of 'em when they were full."

"It's true," Clem said. "Most of these bottles were friends of mine."

Behind the barn lot and corrals, a dry wash marked where the west pasture began. A giant

cottonwood tree had died of old age and lay sprawled in the tall grass, an exposed cut bank behind it. "You go first," I told Clem. "Let's see what you've got."

Carrying the sack that held the cans and bottles, Clem ambled stiff-legged downhill to the fallen tree. Setting four bottles atop the log, he turned and walked back up the slope. Then he turned and faced the targets from a distance of maybe forty feet.

Clem squinted at the bottles, his jaw thrust out and his body posed in what he must have thought was a gunman's crouch. He pulled his forty-five and quickly fired three times from the hip. Shading his eyes, he stared at the log. The bottles stood untouched, shining in the sunlight.

"I guess you just couldn't bear to shoot your friends," I said. "Try again, but take *aim* and shoot this time."

Again, Clem fired three times, his shots aimed and more deliberate than before. I watched the bullets strike the bank beyond the log, but saw one of the bottles explode in a shower of glass.

"You got yourself one 'regulator'," I said, "but you didn't touch the other three. What do you suppose they were doin' while you were missin' them?"

Clem looked rueful. "Killin' me, I reckon."

"I reckon."

I looked at the fallen cottonwood and tried to

clear my mind of all thought save the targets. Taking a deep breath, I let my body go loose and waited for the trigger in my mind. The six-gun seemed to leap into my hand, smacking against my palm as I fired once, twice, three times. Two bottles exploded; the third stood untouched.

"Looks like the 'regulators' got me, too," I said.

"That third feller looked a little cross-eyed," Clem said. "Maybe he *missed* you."

We kept at it. Rusty at first from a lack of practice, my shots began to find their targets. On the other hand, Clem's shots seemed to miss as often as they hit, and then grew worse. Finally, Clem holstered his forty-five and called it a day.

I kept firing, hitting the targets every time at forty feet, then moving back to fifty feet and still hitting a bottle with each shot. When we ran out of bottles, I shot at the cans, rolling them, keeping them moving, jinking them into the air by firing just under them and shooting them on the fly. It was as if I'd never been away.

Clem shook his head and whistled. "By grab, Merlin," he said. "You're *good!*"

I shucked the empty cartridges and reloaded. "I had some pretty good teachers," I said.

"Which brings me to you," I said. "You're still doin' a few things wrong. You're rushin' your shots, shootin' too fast. Keep workin' on hittin' the target every time, and *then* speed up."

"One thing more. No more wearin' that forty-

five to town. Maddox and his boys may prod you into a fight you can't win."

Clem's jaw took on a stubborn set. "Well, now, I wouldn't be so sure about that," he said. "I guess I can hold my temper."

I said nothing, but I guess my face spoke for me. Clem looked at the ground and scuffed it with the toe of his boot. "All right," he said. "Maybe I do have a short fuse. And I reckon I can be prideful sometimes."

"Pride has killed more men than small pox," I said. "Maddox would use your pride to push you."

Clem frowned. "Well," he said, "I sure as hell don't like bein' pushed. Like *you're* pushin' me *now*."

"It's a time for straight talk," I said. "We've got the women to think of."

"All right. I won't wear my forty-five to town."

"I'm obliged, pardner. You're a good man."

"I used to be a better one. Anything else?"

"One more thing," I said. "I think we need to start standin' guard. We wouldn't want those regulators to take us by surprise."

Clem nodded. "No, we wouldn't. How do you figure?"

"I'll stand watch from after supper until two in the mornin'," I said. "You take the second shift from two until daylight."

"Billie will want to do her share."

"Way I see it, Billie and Maggie can watch daylight hours while we're workin'. They can ring the triangle or fire a shot if there's trouble."

"I can see you've thought this out," Clem said. "You sure those regulators will hit us?"

"I'm not sure they *won't*."

Clem offered his hand. "All right, son. It's a deal," he said. "A man could drink to it if he had some whiskey."

"Oh, I expect there's a drop or two around here somewhere. Those bottles didn't get empty by themselves."

Clem laughed. "By grab, you may be right," he said. "Wait here while I see if I can't track down a bottle."

As Clem walked back toward the barn and outbuildings, I breathed a sigh of relief. I had hurt the man's pride and I was sorry, but it was a thing I had to do. In the end, I thought, he had taken it pretty well.

I looked back toward the cottonwood log. My shooting eye had come back. With practice, it would be better.

The mocking voice inside my head returned. *Oh yes,* it said. *You killed some cans* and *bottles today, but of course they weren't men, were they?*

No, I thought. *But if men come, I'll fight.*

Will you? asked the voice. *Or will you see a boy named Toby and turn your hand away?*

I don't know, damn you, I replied.

Nineteen

WHERE THERE'S SMOKE

When the horseman rode into the C Heart, he came not in darkness but in broad daylight. Clem and me had been standing our nightly watches for the better part of a week but had seen no one. And then, just before noon on a hot summer's day, a rider broke out on the ridge of the low hills to the east and turned down toward the home place.

I watched him come, a big man on a blocky roan leading a pack horse behind him. My first thought was that he was a drifter, as I had been, riding the grub line. But as I watched, I had the nagging feeling I *knew* the man, and that I had seen him somewhere before. Jacking a shell into the Winchester's chamber, I walked out to meet him.

I stopped at the east gate and awaited his approach, my rifle at the ready. Seeing me, the rider drew rein and raised his right hand shoulder high and palm out in the old sign of peace. It was then I recognized him—Ross Devlin's cow boss, Sam Bodie!

The big man smiled. "You won't need that saddle gun," he said. "I'm plumb peaceable."

I nodded. "That's good to know, Sam. You here to see Billie?"

"No," he said. "I'm here to see you."

I gave his smile back, but there was no friendly in it. "If that's so, it's hard to believe you're peaceable," I said.

"You mean that little scuffle we had at the barber shop? Hell, you whipped me fair and square. Reckon I had it comin'."

I lowered the rifle. "That's mighty generous," I said. "All right, what can I do for you?"

The big man shifted in his saddle. "I'm here to do somethin' for *you*," he said. "Mind if I step down?"

"Go ahead."

Bodie dismounted. "Is there a shady patch where we can make medicine? There's some things that need sayin'."

"Bunkhouse is yonder. Will that do?"

Bodie loosened the cinch on his saddle and tied both the blue roan and the packhorse to a corral post. He nodded. "Lead the way," he said.

Shaded by the trees and thickets along the river, the bunkhouse was cool and quiet. I led the way inside and sat down at the table near the door. Bodie nodded at the water bucket on the wash stand. "Hot day out yonder. A man gets thirsty."

"Help yourself," I said.

Bodie scooped up a dipper of water and drank long and deep. Then he put the dipper back in the

bucket and sat down across from me. "I've quit the Rafter D," he said. "I'm movin' to new range."

I tried not to show my surprise. "That a fact?" I asked.

"That's a fact. I'm a cow man. I never signed on to run off nesters and hang folks."

"You hung me," I reminded him. "You clubbed me with your rifle and strung me up to a durned tree."

Bodie met my eyes and held them. "I was wrong," he said. "I thought you was a rustler."

"I'd be dead and you'd be *twice* as wrong if that line rider hadn't come along."

The big man nodded, his eyes sad as a bloodhound's. "I owe you, Fanshaw. I'm here to settle accounts."

"If you were part of that Baker hangin', I don't believe you *can*," I said.

"I was no part of that. That was Maddox and his boys."

The bunkhouse cribbage board and our well-used deck of cards sat on the table between us. Bodie reached out and picked up the deck. Riffling the cards, he spread them in a fan. "Cards on the table," he said. "There *ain't* no rustlers to speak of in the Big Open, except them as answers to Ross Devlin. Devlin aims to run all the small operators off the range and take over their land. Some he'll buy out, and some he'll scare out.

Them as don't scare, he'll *burn* out, and claim they're rustlers.

"He aims to take over the C Heart and turn it into the headquarters of a big horse outfit. He wants Billie Hart's ranch and her hot water well, any way he can get 'em. He aims to partner with E. B. Fairfax—they aim to raise thoroughbreds— race horses—and sell 'em to the high rollers back east."

"Why are you tellin' me all this?"

"Ross won't let anything stand in his way. He'll take out anyone he figures is a threat to his plans. *You're* at the top of his list."

"Who else is on that list?"

Bodie made a wry face. "Well, there's me. I'll be watchin' my back trail. Ross just might decide I *know* too much."

"Then I'd say you're burnin' daylight. I appreciate you takin' time to warn me."

Bodie stood up. We shook hands and he walked over to the doorway. Then, as if he suddenly recalled something else he meant to say, he turned back toward me.

"One more thing," he said. "Maddox and his 'regulators' are ridin' today. They aim to kill a *friend* of yours."

"A friend of mine?" I asked.

"I'd say so," Bodie said. "That line rider who saved you from hangin'."

I walked Bodie back to his horses and watched

as he stepped up onto his roan and rode away. Turning, I saw that Billie had come out of the house. She wore her hat low over her eyes and she held her rifle at the ready.

"What did Sam Bodie want?" she asked.

"He's quit the Rafter D," I said. "Says he's had enough of Maddox and those other hard cases. I guess he came here to make amends."

"Wasn't it Sam who tried to hang you the day he found you with the Rafter D steer?"

"It was. He jumped to conclusions that day. He says he's sorry."

Billie continued to watch Bodie and his horses as they grew smaller in the distance.

"And he bears you no ill will for the fight at the barber shop?"

"He says not."

I was beginning to grow restless. If Bodie was telling the truth, Hitch Holbrook was in danger. Maddox and his gunmen would be coming for him with murder on their minds. Someone needed to help him—*I* needed to help him. And yet . . .

"Billie," I said. "Remember Hitch Holbrook, that line rider I told you about? The man who broke up my necktie party that day? Bodie just said the 'regulators' are riding against him today. I don't know whether they plan to kill him out on the range or at his line camp. What I do know is that he'll be alone when they come. I hate to

225

leave you a gun short here, but I'm honor bound to help Hitch if I can."

Billie looked into my eyes, weighing my words. "What if this is a trap? What if Sam told you that story to pull you away from here? What if the C Heart is the real target, or what if they are looking for a chance to catch *you* alone out in the Big Open?"

"Good questions," I said. "I don't have the answers. All I can say is I believe Bodie was tellin' me the truth."

Billie nodded. "All right," she said. "Sam Bodie may be a lot of things, but I never knew him to be untruthful. Go if you must, but be careful. And come back soon. We *need* you around here." Then she paused, and added, "*I* need you."

Minutes later I was mounted on Rutherford, my buckskin, leading Roanie and riding away from the C Heart. At the top of the long ridge above the ranch, I picked up the old wagon road and gave Rutherford his head. Ever eager to see new country, the buckskin set a fast pace. I allowed him to run until he began to labor, and then eased him back to a trot. Hitch Holbrook's line shack was a good fourteen miles away, and I knew I would have to pace my ponies to keep from baking them.

I carried a Winchester in its saddle boot and wore my belted six-gun at my waist. I had no idea

what I might run into at Hitch's, but I believed in being prepared, as best I could. Another six good men at my side would have been a comfort. Barring that, I had good horses and ammunition.

Billie's questions returned to mind as I rode. What if Sam Bodie's story *was* a trap? I had only his word that the regulators planned to kill Holbrook. What made me believe him?

The truth was I had no good reason to believe him at all, and every reason not to. And yet there was something about his words and the simple way he said them that persuaded on a level beyond the mind. Call it a hunch, call it a premonition or a gut feeling, I simply *knew,* and the knowing grew stronger with every minute on the trail.

An hour later, the proof appeared. The fresh tracks of a half-dozen shod horses showed clearly in the road ahead of me. Riders had swept up from the valley, crossed over the ridge, and dropped off into the badlands on the other side. *Maddox and his men!*

I tried to remember how the land laid above the line camp. It had been early morning and still dark when I rode out of there bound for the C Heart, but I recalled that the long ridge north of the cabin ended in a jumble of fallen rock and scrub cedar, yet was clear up to that point. The way the riders had gone was through rough country and deadfall. If I kept to the old road, and

if Maddox and his men were not too far ahead, I might reach Hitch before they did. I touched Rutherford with my spurs and the buckskin broke into a full gallop.

The ridge narrowed. The road grew faint and dropped off to the north, blocking the view of the valley. Where was the slope that led down to the cabin? Could I have missed it?

And then, from across the ridge, I heard the gunfire. Reining the buckskin to a sliding stop, I turned him uphill, searching for a break in the fallen rock and a view of the valley. That's when I smelled the smoke—and a moment later, saw it. Black as ink, it billowed up from below, staining the summer sky and casting a brown shadow as it drifted. Hitch's cabin was ablaze, and the fight was on!

Twenty

CRASHING THE PARTY

Near the crest of the ridge, I piled off Rutherford, pulling the Winchester from its sleeve as I did so. I loose-tied the buckskin to a scrub cedar and secured Roanie's lead rope to my saddle with a half hitch around the horn.

Rocks and loose dirt clattered downhill as I sought to gain a foothold on the steep slope. Scrambling on all fours, I reached the top and surveyed the scene below. A hundred yards away, Hitch's cabin was burning, flames flaring into the sky as if fanned by a blacksmith's bellows. From the cover of a dry wash, half a dozen men were firing with rifles and revolvers at the cabin's door and single window.

On the brushy knoll behind the cabin, two men held the reins of saddle horses after the manner of cavalry fighting on foot. One was a stocky man in a brush jacket. The other—a slim jasper wearing a black hat and a checkered shirt—was Kip Merriday, the self-proclaimed "top hand" and would-be gunfighter I rode with at the C Heart.

Hitch was putting up a fight. After each volley, shots answered from inside the cabin, some accurate enough to make the attackers hug the

ground and hunt for better cover. I saw a dead horse at Hitch's round corral. It looked like the sorrel I'd fitted with horseshoes a few months before.

A man with a rifle stood up from the shelter of the dry wash. He fired three quick shots at the cabin and then dropped into a crouch and ran, maybe to improve his position. An answering shot from the cabin struck him in the thigh and he stumbled, hobbled three or four steps, and fell.

Behind the blazing cabin, I saw movement. The horse holder in the brush jacket handed the reins of the horses to Kip and bent low over what appeared to be some kind of bundle. White smoke drifted up. Carrying the smoking bundle, the man began a slow jog toward the cabin. Sudden awareness came to me as the man ran. He was attacking the cabin from its blind side, and the "bundle" he carried was *dynamite!*

I might have hesitated, but there wasn't time. Centering the rifle's sights on the runner, I squeezed the trigger. The man jerked and toppled forward as my bullet struck him, the bundle flying free. The dynamite exploded with an ear-splitting blast, gouging a hole in the ground just behind the cabin and scattering dirt and smoke in all directions. Frightened by the sound, the horses at the knoll fought their holder, some of them breaking free. I turned my attention to the

attackers in the gulch, firing as fast as I could trigger and lever the Winchester.

Men turned their faces toward me, trying to locate the source of the bullets that struck among them. No longer protected by the dry wash that had shielded them from Hitch's return fire, they panicked. They scrambled out of their trench and made a dash around the cabin, bound for the brushy knoll and their horses.

I caught a glimpse of Maddox. Beneath his black Navajo style hat, the gunman's long white hair whipped like a flag. He was shouting at his men. Maddox pointed uphill in my general direction, but his regulators were more concerned with getting out of harm's way than in shooting back at the ridge from an exposed position. I encouraged their decision by sending another volley of shots their way.

Moving twenty yards or so to a new position on the ridge, I sent several more shots after them as they rushed to get mounted. Horses reared, fighting their riders. Some bolted and fell to bucking. I allowed myself a smile. The ambushers had become the ambushed and it was the last thing they expected. Scrambling and sliding, I hurried down the slope to where I'd left my horses. A moment later I was in the saddle and riding hard toward the burning line shack.

With Roanie following on his lead rope, I spurred Rutherford forward. The horses were

skittish about drawing near the cabin, and Rutherford let me know of his reluctance by rolling his eyes, blowing his nose, and dancing away from the heat and flames. If he'd had the gift of speech I'm sure he would have asked me directly what the hell I thought I was doing. I reined up at the cabin and stepped down.

Smoke and flame poured out through the open door. I tried to look inside, hoping I could catch a glimpse of Hitch, but the smoke caused my eyes to water and I could not. And then suddenly, there he was! Bloodied, and begrimed by smoke, Hitch Holbrook knelt just inside the door, a Winchester carbine in his hands and pointed straight at me!

"Don't shoot, Hitch," I said, "I'm a friend! I'm on *your* side!"

Hitch looked up at me through bloodshot eyes, trying to place me. He coughed, and laid the rifle down. "*Can't* shoot," he said. "No *bullets*." Then he grinned as if he thought being out of cartridges was a great joke.

Helping him to his feet, I led him away from the cabin. "How bad are you hurt?" I asked. "Can you ride?"

"Shot in the leg," he said. "But lucky . . . missed the bone. Hell yes, I can ride."

Hitch stood on his good leg, one arm about my shoulders. His eyes narrowed as he looked down toward his round corral and the dead sorrel.

"Sons o' bitches killed Old Red," he said. "And ran my claybank off."

"You can ride my roan," I said, "but we'd better make tracks. Those regulators might come back."

Hitch showed his teeth in a grimace that was not a smile. "I don't have saddle or bridle," he said. "They burned up in the cabin."

"Good thing *you* didn't. You can ride Roanie bareback, or I will."

"I'll ride him. Just help me get up on him."

Beneath Hitch's shirt, a blood stain grew. "You said you were shot in the leg," I said. "Looks like you took a bullet in your shoulder, too."

Hitch twisted his neck and looked. "Damn!" he said. "I didn't even *know* about that one."

I took off my shirt and tore it down the middle. "Let's patch you up a little," I said, "and then we'll light out."

"Suits me," Hitch said. "Where we goin'?"

"Back to the C Heart, if you can stand it."

"I can stand it," he said. "Let's ride."

And ride we did, south to the long ridge that led to the C Heart and home. We must have made quite a picture—me leading the way on Rutherford, dressed in my ragged old undershirt and carrying Hitch's rifle across the forks of my saddle, and Hitch, bloody and smoke-stained, his calf and his shoulder bandaged with pieces of my

old shirt, riding my Roanie horse bareback. It may well have been a good day to die, as I'm told Indian warriors sometimes declare, but it was an even *better* day to be alive.

When we rode into the C Heart, Clem was on hand to greet us. Clem had been watching from the hayloft of the big barn, and it took him no time at all to climb down and walk out to us. Beside me, Hitch had been drifting in and out of consciousness for the last seven or eight miles, and I knew he was in a bad way. Somehow, he'd managed to stay on Roanie all the way from the line camp, which was quite a feat for a man with two bullet wounds and no saddle.

"Lordamighty!" Clem said. "Looks like you picked a fight with a grizzly and lost! Who's your travelin' companion?"

"Hitch Holbrook. Maddox and his men had him trapped inside his cabin, but he managed to hold 'em off until I showed up. Help me get him inside."

Slowly, Hitch slipped sideways from the roan. His clenched fists held Roanie's mane with a death grip. I had to pry his fingers from their hold before he dropped into Clem's arms.

Hitch was breathing hard and hot as a furnace. Billie and Maggie came hurrying from the house, concern on their faces.

"Put him in my room," Maggie said. "How bad is he hurt?"

"Gunshot wounds. One in the shoulder and one in his lower leg. Minor burns, and lungs full of smoke."

Billie's eyes met mine. "How about you?"

"I'm all right. I managed to get the drop on the bushwhackers. Shot 'em up some from a ridge behind them. They couldn't tell how many men were shootin' so they lit out."

Maggie's room was just off the kitchen, and it was there we took Hitch and laid him in her bed. Maggie looked at Billie. "Put some water on the stove, will you?" she asked. "We'll need to clean him up a bit before I can go to work on his wounds."

Billie nodded. Walking into the kitchen, she built up the fire in the cook stove and put the kettle on. As the water heated, she turned back to Maggie. "Are you sure you can handle this?" she asked. "We could send for the doctor from Fairfax . . ."

Maggie shook her head. "By the time he got here—if a person could find him and if he was sober—you'd need the undertaker. I can take care of this man—with your help."

And during the next hour and twenty minutes, that's just what she did. Maggie sponged the smoke and grime from Hitch's body and applied salve to his burns. The wound to his shoulder was her biggest challenge. The bullet had entered high on the right side of Hitch's chest but had not

passed through. We gave him whiskey and held him down while Maggie probed for, and found, the slug.

Maggie was as gentle as she could be, but we all knew how much Hitch was hurting. The cords of his neck stood out like cables as Maggie carefully removed the bullet and dropped it in a bowl from the kitchen. Sweat silvered Hitch's brow and he clenched his teeth in what he meant to be a smile, but he didn't make a sound.

The wound to Hitch's lower leg was easier, although there was considerable muscle damage. The bullet had passed straight through, and Hitch—and the rest of us—were spared the ordeal of another probing session. Maggie used a turkey baster to rinse the wounds with whiskey, and bandaged them both.

Hitch opened his eyes, looking at Maggie as if she'd hung the moon. I smiled, and said, "I don't guess you two have been introduced. Hitch, say howdy to Maggie Adair. Maggie, meet Hitch Holbrook."

"Proud to know you," Hitch said. "And much obliged."

Maggie tipped the bottle up and took a long drink. "Physician, heal thyself," she said. She began to look for her makin's but while she was working on Hitch I'd borrowed her tobacco and papers. I presented a fresh-rolled cigarette to both Maggie and Hitch and struck a match. "Nice

work, Doctor Adair," I said. "Where did you learn to do that?"

"Do what?" she asked. "Drink whiskey? Or patch up wounded men?"

Maggie took a deep drag on her cigarette, and exhaled blue smoke. "I told you about my late husband," she said. "He kept my life interesting, but he did pick up a few bullets during his short life."

Outside, I found that Clem had already taken care of my horses. "There was so much blood on your roan that I thought he surely must be wounded," Clem said. "Turned out it all belonged to that cowhand you brought home. Is he the man who saved you from hangin'?"

"That's him," I said. "I figure those gunslingers went after him out of pure meanness, because he helped me."

Briefly, I told Clem about the raid on the line camp and the short skirmish with Hitch's attackers. His eyes shone when I told him how I'd ambushed the ambushers.

"Sounds like you bloodied their nose a bit," he said.

"I crashed the party," I said. "The only man that I know I shot was the man with the dynamite. I stopped him before he could blow the cabin, but I don't know what happened after that. And I saw Hitch drop one shooter from his cabin door. I saw no dead or wounded when we left. Whatever

casualties the bushwhackers suffered went out when they did."

Clem was silent for a time. He looked off at the distant hills, maybe seeing the skirmish at the line camp in his imagination. Then he said, "What do you figure will happen next?"

"Maddox and his men will come," I said. "Especially if they find out I broke up their ambush and that Hitch Holbrook is here. Ross Devlin wants this ranch like a drownin' man wants dry. He's not about to just walk away and let us alone."

"No, he's not," Clem said. "But it ain't a matter of *if* they find out, it's a matter of *when.* Somehow, word always gets out."

Twenty-One
SHOPPING, INTERRUPTED

Next morning when I showed up at the main house, Maggie sat at her usual place beside the stove, a cup of coffee in her hands and a cigarette dangling from her lips. The table was set, and the good smells of coffee, hotcakes, and bacon gave evidence that breakfast was ready, as it was every morning. In fact, everything seemed the same that morning except Maggie herself.

Dark circles beneath her eyes and a pinched look about her mouth gave Maggie a weary, careworn appearance. I favored her with my best smile. "Good mornin', Maggie!" I said. "You're pretty as a sunrise today!"

Maggie squinted against the cigarette smoke and said, "Well, it's *morning* all right but I'm not sure how *good* it is. I was up most of the night tending to our house guest."

Maggie poured a cup of coffee from the pot on the stove and handed it to me. "He came down with a fever at about one o'clock. Night sweats, raving in his sleep, throwing off his blankets. It sounded like he was reliving the fight at the line shack. I gave him a little sage tea and whiskey, and wiped him down with some cool cloths.

239

Along about four this morning he finally fell asleep."

"What about his wounds?"

"He'll be sore for awhile, but I don't expect that will keep him down."

Billie walked in from the other side of the house. Smiling, she said, "If I read his brand correctly, he'll probably want to be horseback by this afternoon. Good morning, Merlin."

"Mornin', Billie. Maggie says she's not sure if it's a *good* mornin' or not."

Maggie shrugged. She said, "One gal's 'good morning' is another gal's 'good god, it's morning.'"

I sipped my coffee. "Hitch will need a bedroll and some work clothes," I said. "I think I'll go into Fairfax today. I'll pick him up a few things."

Just then Clem walked in. "You're goin' *where?*" he asked. "What if you run into Maddox and his boys? After yesterday, they'll buy you a quick trip to the bone orchard!"

I held up three fingers. "Three things," I said. "First, they're not likely to *be* in town today. More likely they're back in the hills somewhere, lickin' their wounds and tryin' to figure out what happened. Second, nobody *saw* me yesterday. Those boys don't know who fired at them or how many shooters there were."

"And third," I said. "They're not likely to hit us here at the C Heart until they get themselves

organized, so today is the safest time for me to be away."

Clem wasn't convinced. "I wish I was as sure of all that as you are," he said. "Well, if you're goin' in, I'll come *with* you. You might need a good man to back your play."

I shook my head. "Afraid not, Clem. Billie and Maggie need a good man *here* just in case I'm wrong."

Billie frowned. "Any *other* reason you want to go into Fairfax?"

"All right. Yes, there is. I thought I'd try to get word of the raid on Hitch's line shack to the sheriff's office at Miles City. There might still be time to head off a showdown."

Billie still looked uncertain. Turning to Maggie, she asked, "Well? What do you think, Mag? Shall we let this loco cowpoke go into town?"

"I suppose," Maggie said. She raised her eyes to mine. "But I'll be mighty *upset* if you get yourself hurt or killed there. And cowboy, you don't want to *see* an upset *Maggie Adair!*"

Down at the big corral, I ran in some of the horses in my string and cut out Old Ebenezer, the black gelding I'd rode pulling bog. Rutherford and Roanie needed a day or two of rest, and I figured Ebenezer could see me through most anything I chanced to encounter, from a rattle-snake convention to a small war.

I dabbed a loop on him with my catch rope, and

he came along easy. Ten minutes later, he was saddled, bridled, and ready to go. I untracked him in the road outside the corral, stepped up on him, and waved to Billie, Maggie, and Clem. With a touch of my spur, Old Ebenezer set sail for Fairfax.

I rode light in the stirrups on the way. Each thicket I passed, each grove of trees, and every dry wash and coulee that could hide a man with a rifle received my full attention that morning. I don't know; maybe it was the shoot-out at the line camp that had me spooking at shadows, but I kept my eyes on the hilltops and on the road ahead, feeling like a duck in a shooting gallery.

I was nowhere near as confident of my safety as I'd made out. What I told Billie and Maggie was true enough. Maddox and his gunmen *would* likely be hunkered down after their failed raid. And it *wasn't* likely they knew I had a hand in running them off. But they might have left a man up in the hills to keep an eye on the C Heart. If so, they could know all our comings and goings, including the two-man parade Hitch and me put on when we came back to Billie's place the night before.

Still, I figured the trip was worth the risk. As county sheriff, Tom Irvine needed to know of the troubles in the Big Open and take a hand. And as much as I wished that could be someone else's

job, I knew it was mine. And so, two hours after leaving the ranch I turned Ebenezer down onto the main street of Fairfax.

I rode past the Grand Hotel and the Mint Saloon, paying particular attention to the horses that were tied out front. I counted eight at the hitch rack off the hotel's broad veranda, but none of them wore Rafter D brands. Across the street at the Mint, three cow ponies slept in the sunshine, only their restless tails seemingly awake as they switched flies away. I recognized two of their brands. They didn't belong to Devlin's outfit, either.

Drawing rein at the Fairfax Mercantile, I stepped down. I loose-tied Ebenezer to the rack, stepped up onto the raised walkway, and went inside. Behind the counter, the storekeeper raised his eyes from the ledger he was keeping and smiled. Recognizing me, his smile faded.

"Good morning," he said. "What can I do you for, cowboy?"

"Need a few things," I said. "Pair of waist overalls for a tall feller. Taller than me. Two work shirts for the same. One shirt for me. And one undershirt."

The storekeeper busied himself at the shelves, and then laid the items I'd asked for on the counter. "These overalls are a good buy," he said. "They're made of heavy nine-ounce brown duck, with a double seat and double fabric down

the inside legs. Perfect for a horseman. Ninety-eight cents a pair. The shirts are blue flannel, three for two-seventy-five. Undershirt is forty-five cents."

He made a quick calculation with pencil and paper. "That'll be four dollars and eighteen cents," he said. "Will there be anything else?"

"Four boxes of cartridges. Forty-four forty."

Behind his eyeglasses, the storekeeper blinked. He frowned. Sweat broke out on his upper lip, "I . . . I don't believe I have that caliber," he said.

"*Sure* you do," I said.

The storekeeper couldn't meet my eyes. He lowered his gaze to the counter top. In the stillness, I heard the buzzing of a fly. From somewhere in the store came the measured ticking of a clock.

The storekeeper picked up his pencil again and did another quick calculation. Then he cleared his throat and said, "Cartridges are seventy cents a box. Your total is six dollars and ninety-eight cents."

I took off my gun belt and laid it on the counter. The storekeeper turned white. My cartridge belt, like many others at the time, doubled as a money belt. I fished out a ten-dollar gold eagle and handed it to him.

"As I recall, you're not too big on credit sales," I said.

The storekeeper's face turned red, starting at his

celluloid collar. He made no reply, but took the coin and handed back the difference. "Three dollars and two cents," he said.

He wrapped the shells and dry goods in paper and tied the bundle with string. His smile was weak as he handed the package to me. "How is Miss Billie?" he asked.

"Fine as frog hair," I said. "Of course, she's *always* fine. Miss Billie is a fine lady."

"Uh . . . Yes. Yes, she certainly is. I appreciate your business. And hers, of course."

I buckled on my gun belt on and turned toward the door. "I'll tell her you said so, pardner. Tap 'er light."

"Tap 'er what?"

"Just somethin' the miners say over at Butte. Means 'take it easy.' "

And I walked out into the sunlight.

Outside, I wrapped the package inside my slicker and tied it behind the cantle of my saddle. I still had one more stop to make, and I rode Ebenezer down to the hotel and tied him up out in front.

When I crossed the lobby, I saw that the same desk clerk I'd met previously was on duty. He was still playing solitaire, and his attitude had not improved.

"I wish you damn cowpunchers would tidy up a bit before you come in here," he said. "Every

time I deal with one of you knights of the plains, I have to sweep up the trail dust you leave behind."

"Yeah. That must cut in on your card playin' considerable. Does it still cost a dollar to telephone Miles City?"

"Telephone's out of commission," he said. "Every telephone in town. A line must be down somewhere."

"That's too bad. Are these telephones only out of commission for me, or for everybody?"

"For everybody."

"Even for Ross Devlin?"

A voice behind me said, "Even for me."

I turned quickly and found myself face to face with Ross Devlin. My hand dropped to my holstered Colt, but a sharp nudge against my spine told me I was too late. "Stand easy, Deputy," a cold voice said. "This ain't a play you can win."

I raised my hands and turned my head. The man called Maddox drew my gun from its leather and smiled a cold smile. "Sorry we missed each other at the line camp yesterday," he said. "You broke up our party."

Deputy, Ross had called me. It appeared my past had caught up with me. And how did Maddox know I'd been at the line camp? I was surprised and flummoxed, but I wasn't going to let Devlin and Maddox know that.

"I didn't mean to be impolite," I said. "But I thought you boys were playin' a mite *rough* with the guest of honor."

Beneath the wide brim of his Stetson, Devlin's face was a hard mask. "The regulators threw a party for Holbrook," he said. "Now I'll throw one for *you*—back at the Rafter D."

Devlin frowned. "I just came back from Miles City last night," he said. "Kid at Ringer's Livery told me an interesting story while I was there. Seems the county sheriff and a U.S. deputy marshal broke up a bank robbery there earlier this year. This deputy gunned down the horse holder. Killed him outright. Only then he found out the horse holder wasn't armed, and that he was only a simple-minded boy. Deputy's name was Merlin Fanshaw, same as yours. Hell of a coincidence, don't you think?"

"Sure is," I said. "Whatever happened to the deputy?"

"They say he turned in his badge and rode off into the Big Open. I think maybe he signed on as a cowhand with the C Heart spread."

Devlin's eyes narrowed to slits. His mouth tightened in a grim line.

"You've been a thorn in my side ever since you hit this country," he said. "You've got in the way of my plans and you've turned Billie Hart against me."

"Hell, Devlin," I said. "*You* turned Billie against

you. Like most women, she'd rather hear straight talk from a man than sweet talk from a skunk."

Devlin's face flushed. His eyes blazed. For a moment I thought he was going to lose control, but he hobbled his temper and kept the lid on. His smile was cold as a blizzard. "The only reason I don't kill you right now is that I need to know the answer to a question," he said. "Did you quit the marshal's service, or are you working undercover?"

"I know you made a telephone call to the sheriff's office in Miles City. What did you tell Tom Irvine?"

"I don't recall," I said.

"That's all right. We'll take a ride out to the Rafter D, where we can talk more freely. And believe me, you *will* recall.

"Walk slow and easy out that door. After I'm mounted, Maddox will tell you to step up on that sturdy black you're riding. Then Maddox will mount up, and we'll all ride out to the ranch together, like pumpkin rollers going to church.

"Try anything—anything at all—and I'll be explaining to the city marshal how I had to cut you down in self defense when you tried to jump me. He will believe me. He's the best town marshal I ever owned."

Outside, a bearded rider on a flea-bit grey held the reins of two saddled horses. The man was

a hard-looking *hombre*, dark of skin and wearing a black patch over his right eye. He smiled a thin smile when he saw us come out of the hotel.

Ross Devlin's silver mounted saddle sat atop one of the led horses. The other, a coyote dun, I figured was Maddox's mount. My horse, the black gelding called Ebenezer, stood at the hitch rack where I'd left him.

Maddox looped my cartridge belt and holstered gun over his saddle horn and nudged me in the back with his own revolver. "Get mounted," he said. "And no tricks."

I stepped up into my saddle. Ross Devlin rode up on my right. He said, "In case you're wondering how I knew you'd be here today, the answer is easy. My man 'One Eye' Jackson over there has been watching the C Heart for days now. He's a mute—he doesn't speak—but he sees better with one eye than most men see with two. 'One Eye' saw you and Holbrook come back from the line shack shootout. And he watched you ride out this morning. As soon as I heard you were on the road to Fairfax, we rode in to greet you."

"Neighborly of you," I said. "I sure hope you didn't go to any trouble."

Devlin frowned. "Trouble? You've caused me nothing *but* trouble!"

His eyes blazed. "There's a shallow grave waiting for you at the Rafter D," he said. "You

know why we dug it shallow? So the coyotes can get their teeth in you quicker!"

With a slash of his quirt, Devlin rode out ahead of Maddox, One Eye, and me. I took a deep breath and tried to put my mind to work. For maybe the thousandth time in my life, I couldn't help wishing I was as brave as I talked.

Twenty-Two

IN ENEMY HANDS

The road to the Rafter D was a dusty wagon track through windblown grass. It wound northwest, leaving Powder River behind and twisting through broken coulees and rocky hills. Just ten miles from Billie's place by way of the Mizpah Creek trail, the headquarters of the Rafter D was located near the junction of Powder River and Ash Creek. I knew about the site from the descriptions of others, but I had never been there. Now I was going there, but it wasn't my idea.

One Eye Jackson and Maddox rode behind me, and it almost seemed I could feel their hard eyes fixed on my back.

Ross Devlin led the way, sitting tall and straight in the saddle. After our brief exchange as we left town, he didn't speak to me again. That was more than all right with me. I needed time to think, time to plan.

Beneath me, Ebenezer kept pace with Devlin's thoroughbred, moving at an easy dog trot. Suppose I made a break for it? Could the big-chested black carry me to safety? My holstered gun and belt were looped over Maddox's saddle horn. Maddox had taken my Winchester and now

rode with it across the forks of his saddle. No, I didn't like the odds. I would bide my time. My chance would come. *Please God, let it come.*

Time seemed to slow down to a snail's pace. As the miles rolled by, I tried to think of a way to get free of Devlin and his men, but I could not. I knew in a general way what was in store for me when we reached the Rafter D, and I was not looking forward to it.

And then it was too late. Ahead of me, Ross Devlin reined up at a barbed wire gate and waited. One Eye Jackson rode past and dismounted. He opened the gate and held it as Devlin rode through. I glanced up. A sign dangled from the ridge pole atop the gateposts:

Rafter D – Devlin Ranch — No Trespassing.

"Ride on through, Deputy," Maddox said. "That 'no trespass' sign don't apply to dead men." I slacked my rein and rode Ebenezer through the gate. Maddox came after, holding the rifle on me as if he hoped I'd try to escape. One Eye closed the gate behind us, mounted his flea bit grey, and brought up the rear.

Ahead, the road dropped off into a green and sunlit valley. Buildings lay scattered across the flat like poker dice on a bar top. Atop a hill, a two-story ranch house commanded a view of the valley floor. Below, on a gentle slope, was a sod-roofed bunkhouse, a log barn, a round corral, and a blacksmith shop. Ross led the way to the shop

252

and waited until we caught up. Speaking to Maddox, he said, "I'm going up to the house for a minute," he said. "I'll be back directly."

"What do you want us to do with Fanshaw?" Maddox asked.

"Take him inside and fire up the forge. There's nothing like a hot iron to loosen a man's tongue."

One Eye Jackson tied my black and his flea bit grey to a hitch rack outside the shop. Maddox stepped off his coyote dun and left the animal free to graze on the tall grass nearby. I looked up toward the bunkhouse. Kip Merriday was coming toward us like a man in a hurry. Ross turned his horse and met him. Drawing rein, he spoke to Kip. "Who all is up at the bunkhouse, Kip?"

"Everybody but Al and Whiskey Bill, Mr. Devlin," Kip said. "The boys have a big poker game goin'. You want me to call 'em out?"

"No," Ross said. "We can do what we need to without them. Go help Maddox."

Touching his thoroughbred with his spurs, Ross rode away toward the big house. Maddox watched him ride away, and turned his attentions to me. Holding me by my shirt front, he shoved me through the shop's open door.

"Now, you lawdog sonofabitch," he said, "you got two of my men killed at the line shack yesterday, and we're about to settle accounts!"

One Eye stepped inside. He held his six-gun at the ready, a wolfish grin on his face. Kip

Merriday looked at Maddox the way a sheepdog looks at the shepherd.

"What do you want me to do?" he asked.

"Fire up the forge," Maddox said. "Ross aims to learn this lawdog how to sing."

Maddox pushed me down on the shop's floor and tied my hands behind me. Rolling over, I struggled to my knees.

"I've got a whiskey bottle up at the bunkhouse," Maddox said. "I'm goin' up to fetch it. Then I'll be back for the concert."

I didn't see it coming. Maddox turned away, and then suddenly stepped back and caught me in the belly with a savage kick. Pain shot through me like a flame. I fell face down to the floor and lay there gasping for air. Through the open door I watched Maddox's dun grazing, his bridle reins trailing in the grass.

Maddox should have tied him up, I thought. *He sure wouldn't want him to wander off* . . .

I smiled through the pain. *I'm* tied up, I thought. Not much danger *I'll* wander off.

One Eye hunkered down near the door, rolling himself a smoke. He seemed indifferent to my plight, concerned only with shaping his cigarette. To take my mind off the ache in my gut and the torment yet to come, I made a survey of the shop.

It was like many another ranch blacksmith shop. I lay on oil-stained planks amid the scraps and debris of previous work. A forge with a gear-

driven blower stood on a base of old brick. A hood and a pipe connection were in place to take away the smoke. The hearth was heaped with blacksmithing coal and coke, ash and clinkers. An anvil stood near the forge, mounted on a cross section of a cottonwood tree.

Behind me, tongs, hammers, and assorted chisels and punches littered the top of a rough workbench. Branding irons, horseshoes, mowing machine sickles, log chains, and rusty scrap iron of every kind filled the corners of the shop and littered the floor. I leaned back, resting on my tightly bound hands.

Kip picked up the forge shovel and approached the hearth. He looked at me with what might have been mixed feelings and said, "Well, what do you say *now*, Fanshaw? You ain't so high and mighty *now*, are you?"

I made no reply, but I had to admit that high and mighty did not describe my feelings at that moment.

Kip began to clean the fire bowl, pushing all the coal and coke back on the hearth and throwing out the clinkers. "You should have quit the C Heart when I did," he said. "Ridin' high with the Regulators beats the hell out of pullin' cows out of the mud."

"Now it's too late for you," he said. "Turns out you're some kind of a lawman spy, tryin' to bring trouble to a great man like Mr. Devlin." Kip

shook the fine cinders and ashes through the grate and into the ash pit.

"I've got *friends* now," Kip said. "I'm runnin' with *pistoleros*—sure enough real professional gun fighters like Mr. Maddox. Admit it—old Kip Merriday has done pretty well for himself."

I found I could breathe again. "Hell, Kip. Maddox doesn't give a damn about you. You're just his errand boy. A man doesn't have to call a friend 'mister'."

"Shut up! You don't know what you're talkin' about! Mr. Maddox and me are partners!"

"He'll sell you out, Kip. Wait and see."

"*You* wait and see," Kip said. "Mr. Maddox will be back soon, and *then* you'll find out."

Kip turned the hand crank on the blower, making sure a good gust of air came through. Then he lit a small handful of wood shavings and dropped them in the tube that carried air to the forge. I looked away as fire was kindled in the hearth.

And then I caught a break.

Behind me in the grit and litter of the floor, my fingers closed on a scrap from some earlier forge work—a short, sharp-edged piece of steel. Across from me, One Eye smoked, watching me by way of his good eye.

Sawing with the piece of steel, I began to work on the ropes that bound me. In the darkness, I nicked my wrist and felt a sharp stab of pain.

Shoulders aching from the forced position of my bound hands, I kept rubbing away. The sound of the blower at the forge covered any sound my efforts might have made, and I kept my mind on my task.

A strand gave way! And then another! My heartbeat was pulsing in my ears. My mouth was dry, but the palms of my hands were wet. The steel cut through the *third* strand! My hands were *free!*

Moving slow and easy, I got to my feet. Across from me, One Eye had turned away to roll another cigarette. I turned toward the forge, where Kip was busy stirring the coals in the hearth. He didn't see me as I slowly rose to my feet.

Kip must have caught movement from the corner of his eye. He stepped back from the forge to face me, his eyes wide and staring. The forge shovel dropped with a clang and a clatter, and Kip reached for the revolver on his right hip.

His gun was out of the leather and coming up. I had turned my back on One Eye, but a quick glance told me he was coming for me. I jerked to the side just as the blast of Kip's gun shattered the silence. I heard the bullet's impact as it burned past my belly and struck One Eye dead center!

My left hand closed on Kip's gun as he cocked its hammer for a second shot. Tearing the weapon from his hand, I caught him full in the face with

my right fist. Thrown backward, Kip tripped over the anvil and sprawled full length.

Outside, Maddox's coyote dun still grazed on the tall grass. The gelding raised its head as I came running from the shop. *Don't spook,* I thought. *Don't shy, boy.*

Head held high and his nostrils flaring, the dun danced a nervous quick-step as I approached. "Easy, big horse," I said. "Easy now."

Up the slope, men had heard the gunshot and were coming out of the bunkhouse. Walking back to the shop, Maddox dropped his whiskey bottle and pulled his revolver. He started to run.

My own gun and shell belt were still on the forks of Maddox's saddle. Tucking Kip's pistol in my waistband, I bent low and picked up a trailing bridle rein. My left foot found the nigh stirrup. The coyote dun broke into a run as I grasped the saddle horn with my right hand. Then I was mounted and riding fast away from the outbuildings of the Rafter D.

Pistol shots broke out behind me, but I knew we were out of range and picking up speed. Pursuit would come soon enough, I thought. Devlin and Maddox, and every "regulator" on the place would be horseback and hot on my heels. But I was free and well mounted, and I struck out for the trail that would take me back to the C Heart. It was enough for the moment, and more than I'd hoped.

Ahead, a three-wire fence loomed. I slacked the dun's reins, bent low over his neck, and gave him his head. The big horse cleared the fence by inches, and we struck out for Billie's place at a full gallop.

Twenty-Three
THE WELCOMING COMMITTEE

The coyote dun carried me away from the Rafter D at a breakneck pace, twisting and dodging through broken country and sagebrush as tall as a man. Some horses run because their riders require it and some because it is their nature. I was relieved and plumb encouraged finding that the dun ran simply because he *loved* to.

On my desperate flight that afternoon, I rode a borrowed—all right, *stolen*—horse about which I knew nothing. Considering my life was in the balance you can understand my delight at having found a mount that ran like the very wind.

Not that my ride was without a difficulty or two. Shortly after we cleared the three-wire fence, the dun commenced to run and buck with an exuberance that tested my horsemanship and troubled my mind. I made a good ride, although I choked the horn and clawed leather without shame. Considering the shallow grave that waited for me back at the ranch and the nature of the men who pursued me, I would have stayed in the saddle if it had been on fire.

For the first mile, I allowed the dun to run flat

out, reining him back to a lope when he began to labor. Another mile and I rode him to a hilltop just off the trail and allowed him to blow. Looking back the way I'd come, I saw no signs of close pursuit but I knew I was not out of the woods by any means. Ross Devlin rode a thoroughbred that could quickly close the gap, and most of the Rafter D horses I'd seen were clear-footed saddlers that could stay the course.

I touched the dun with my spurs and the animal didn't hesitate. The big horse took me straight down the hillside, stiff-legged and heedless. Loose dirt and rock cascaded around us, and I shoved my feet forward in the stirrups and leaned far back in order to help in our descent.

Once we were back on the trail, I sent the gelding into a hard gallop again, alternating every mile or so with a ground-covering trot. We proceeded like this on our way back to Billie's place.

I had no doubt but that Ross Devlin would come after us. Billie had frustrated his every attempt to acquire the C Heart, but I knew Ross had not given up, not by a jugful. He would come, and he would bring Maddox and his gunmen with him. Billie's place, and the artesian well it contained, were essential to Ross's plans. He would not take no for an answer.

As to when he would come, I believed it would be soon. Maybe, like the raid on the Baker

homestead, riders would come in the dark of night to burn Billie out. Or maybe they were dogging my trail even then, mere minutes behind me. All I knew was that I had to reach the C Heart and warn my friends. Slacking my rein and leaning forward over the withers of the dun, I broke him out of his trot and into a full gallop again.

The sun was low in the sky when I rode down the ridge east of the C Heart. I had come the way Sam Bodie came, along Mizpah Creek and then down the slope to the ranch's east gate. As I stepped off the lathered dun to open the gate, Clem Guthrie appeared in the distance out of the shadows of the barn loft, shading his eyes as he watched me. I was pleased. Clem was on guard.

And then suddenly my mood changed. Splinters exploded from the gatepost just inches from my hand, and the sharp crack of a Winchester broke the stillness. Clem was firing at me! I had no white flag nor could I make myself heard at that distance, so I did the next best thing. I raised both hands and waved like a Holy Roller at a camp meeting. There was a heap less "hallelujah" to my gesture than there was "don't shoot." I prayed Clem would accept my surrender.

Leading the dun, I closed the gate behind me and started walking up the lane toward the barn and outbuildings. Again, I saw Clem shade his eyes against the sun. Closer by then, I called out,

"Hold your fire, Clem! It's me . . . it's Merlin!"

Clem disappeared from the open loft and walked out the big door on the ground level. Still holding the Winchester at the ready, he took a few steps toward me. "Merlin?" he yelled.

"By grab," he said. "It *is* you! What are you doin' comin' home by the east gate instead of the town road? And where's the horse you rode out on . . . where's Ebenezer?"

Concern was plain on Clem's face. He'd nearly shot me, and he was rattled. I took hold of his shoulder and squeezed.

"I'll tell you while we walk," I said. "I sure am glad you didn't shoot me. We both would have felt terrible."

"Well, how was *I* to know it was you? Leave here on a black horse, come back on a coyote dun . . ."

"All's well, Clem. Glad to see you're on the job. Now let's go find Billie and the others. There's a storm comin' fast from the Rafter D, and we need to hold another war council."

We gathered together around the coffee boiler—Maggie, Billie, Clem, Hitch, and me. Maggie had bandaged Hitch's shoulder and thigh, and the line rider's face was haggard and somber. He sat in a chair with his right arm in a sling and listened intently to my every word.

I told it all. I recounted the shooting of Toby Slocum back in Miles City, and how I had walked

away from my life as a lawman. I told them of my recent trip to Fairfax, and of meeting Ross Devlin, Maddox, and One Eye Jackson at the hotel.

I spoke of my forced ride to the Rafter D and Ross's desperation. "Ross is not the man you thought you knew," I said. "His greed and ambition have made him ruthless."

Billie said nothing, but she held her head high and met my eyes with her own level gaze. There was both reluctance and resolve in her expression, like a dutiful child accepting a dose of bad-tasting medicine.

"Ross wants your place, and he has schemed with E. B. Fairfax and the bank to force you to sell to him. The C Heart, and especially your artesian well, is fundamental to his plan—he wants to develop a first class stud farm here for thoroughbreds.

"His so-called war on rustling is just an excuse to run small ranchers and nesters off their land. Sam Bodie told me there *is* no rustling in the Big Open, or very little. Ross brought in Maddox and his gun hands to take over the range and to serve as his private army.

"They lynched Irv Baker and they burned the Bakers' house. And it wasn't just Maddox and his men getting out of hand. I have proof that Ross was with them that night.

"After Irv's funeral, I made a telephone call to Tom Irvine to tell him what I knew. Tom was

away at the time but I spoke to his deputy. Ross heard about the telephone call and got nervous. The scriptures say, 'The guilty flee when no man pursueth,' and I guess that applies to Ross.

"He was worried about what I might have told the sheriff, so he was fixin' to torture me some and find out. After that, he said he'd kill me and plant me in a shallow grave somewhere on the Rafter D. I didn't approve of his arrangements, so I borrowed Maddox's horse and lit out."

"Glad you did," Maggie said. "But why did they go after Hitch?"

"Hitch broke up their party that day they strung me up for rustling," I said. "The attack on Hitch was a *revenge* raid. Ross doesn't *like* havin' his power challenged."

In the silence that followed, no one spoke. Maggie rolled a smoke for Hitch and lit it for him. Clem pursed his lips and frowned into his coffee cup. Billie walked to the front windows and looked out toward the eastern hills. And I, having said all, waited.

Billie turned back from the windows. "All right," she said. "What do we do?"

I shrugged. "That's for you to say, Billie. Whatever we do, we need to do it fast."

"You think they'll hit us tonight?"

I nodded. "This afternoon. Tonight. Tomorrow morning at the latest."

Clem spoke up. "How *many* do you figure?"

"Ten or twelve, maybe. Including Ross himself."

Hitch cleared his throat. "They're after you and me, Merlin. I say Clem should take the ladies and ride out. Maybe hole up in town."

Clem stood up. "And *I* say I ain't a-goin' *no where!* No raggedy-ass pack of night riders is runnin' *me* off this place! I aim to stay here and *fight!*"

Maggie smiled, and was suddenly beautiful. "For once, the feisty old fool is right," she said. "I agree with Clem. The C Heart is my home."

Billie smiled and walked toward me. "And mine," she said. "We're all staying. And we'll all fight."

She looked into my eyes, and the trust I saw there was a burden almost too heavy to bear. "This sort of business is more your line than ours," she said. "Tell us what to do, Deputy."

I swallowed hard. "Well," I said. "The first thing we have to do is take inventory. How many rifles do we have?"

"Three," Clem said. "We had four, but you got careless and left yours at the Rafter D."

"We still have four," I said. "Maddox has a Winchester on the horse I stole. I'm glad *we've* got it instead of him."

I looked at Hitch. "How about you, pardner? Can you handle a rifle?"

"You bet," he said. "I'll have to shoot left-handed, but I'll manage."

"Revolvers?" I asked. "I count four—Clem's, Hitch's, mine, and a nickel-plated pistol we've seen before. I 'borrowed' it from Kip Merriday today."

"You surely do a heap of borrowin'," Clem said. "'Borrowed' Maddox's horse, 'borrowed' that pimp's pistol of Kip's. I don't know about you, son."

"Give it to Billie," Maggie said. "I'll make out with my scattergun."

"All right," I said. "Anything else?"

"Like what?" Clem asked. "A Gatlin' gun? A Mountain Howitzer? We ain't got . . ."

"Whoa, Nellie!" he said. "There *is* somethin'! We've got most of a case of *dynamite* down in the tool shed!"

"Dynamite?" I asked.

"Nothin' but! I used it last year to blow some beaver dams out of the creek! We've got blastin' caps and fuses, too!"

I took Clem by the arm. "Show me," I said.

The tool shed at the C Heart was a catch-all of rusty tools, miscellaneous hardware, and dust. Coils of rope and wire hung from pegs on the walls. Partial rolls of tar paper, old canvas, and oil cloth occupied the cluttered floor. Against the shed's back wall, dusty shelves held coffee cans filled with assorted nails, staples, nuts, and bolts. And a wooden box with dove-tailed corners marked "DYNAMITE – 50 LBS 1 1/4″ x 8″."

"There she is," Clem said. "As I recall, that box is nearly full!"

Carefully, Clem slid the box off the shelf and placed in on the floor. Removing the lid, he turned the open box toward sunlight. Dynamite sticks lay in ordered rows, like the Devil's cigars.

"What did I tell you?" Clem asked. "I've got blastin' caps, too."

Crystals of nitroglycerine showed on some of the sticks. I cleared my throat. "Some hard rock miners in Butte told me the shelf life of dynamite is about a year," I said. "How long have you had this box?"

Clem shrugged. "Maybe a year and a half. That just means we'll need to be a mite more careful."

"We'll need three or four bundles, eight sticks to a bundle. We'll wrap each bundle with twine, and attach blasting caps."

Within a few minutes, the bundles were prepared. I picked up a shovel from the tools in the corner. "Bring the bundles and follow me," I said. "Try not to stumble."

"You've got a real gift for givin' unnecessary advice," Clem said.

Twenty-Four
RECEIVING VISITORS

The sun set slowly that evening, as if reluctant to end the day. It seemed to hover above the far horizon for awhile before it settled below the edge of the world and set the clouds on fire. Birds of the day fell silent and took to their nests. Frogs held sober discussions along the creek banks. Twilight came, and with it the false promise of peace and rest, for there would be neither that night at the C Heart.

We met again in the kitchen. Every eye was turned to me for assurance and hope, but I had little to give. All through the afternoon we had watched and waited for Devlin's men to come riding against us, but they had not.

On the one hand, I was grateful for the delay. It gave us time to prepare, to set up our defenses as best we could. I had believed the riders would show up before sundown. Now darkness was falling. Would they come during the night?

Billie's brown eyes were troubled. "Maybe they're not coming at all," she said. "Maybe Ross has changed his mind."

"They're coming," I said. "Tonight in the dark or tomorrow in the daylight. They're coming for

Hitch and me, if nothing else. Ross will come because he *has* to."

"Let's go over our plan one more time," I said. "Clem will watch from the hayloft, as before. If the riders come by way of Mizpah Creek or from the south, Clem will see them.

"Billie, Maggie, and Hitch will defend the house. Both Billie and Hitch have rifles. Ring the ranch triangle if you have time, and open fire from the windows. The riders will be moving fast, so take careful aim and don't forget to lead them. Make every shot count.

"I'll be on the ridge behind the house. I'll have a good view of the bridge and the road to the west, as well as all that open country to the north.

"This afternoon, Clem and me planted dynamite charges at the east gate, the hillside above the bridge, the barn lot, and across the creek at the hay meadows. Each of the charges are capped, so a well-aimed shot at any one of them should provide a good imitation of artillery."

"And a nasty surprise for Ross and his night riders," Maggie said.

"That's the plan," I said.

Outside, dusk had turned to darkness. Stars winked on in the moonless sky. Billie turned the lamp down low and settled in with her rifle beside the east-facing window. Hitch moved his chair to the covered front porch and sat overlooking the

cottonwood grove and hay meadows beyond the creek. Clem crossed the open lot and disappeared into the deep shadows of the barn and out-buildings.

Earlier, I had saddled Rutherford and tied him out behind the bunkhouse. *You never know,* I thought. *This could become a running fight.*

I took a blanket from my bedroll, my old Army binoculars, and Maddox's Winchester and hiked up the trail behind the house. When I reached the top of the ridge, I chose a vantage point in a patch of scrub cedar and hunkered down to wait.

It's going to be a long and sleepless night, I thought.

Some folks hear nothing in the night save silence, but the world after dark has sounds aplenty. Far away, out on the plain, coyotes sang their lonesome song. Somewhere in the upper pasture, a cow called to her calf. From an old dead tree behind the bunkhouse, an owl asked its age-old question. *Who? Who-who?*

I thought: *Our little five-person army has an owl standing guard. Halt, he's saying. Who-who goes there?*

A cool breeze blew up from the creek, bringing the rich smells of warm earth and curing hay. In the stillness, the patter of the leaves on the cottonwood trees made a sound like falling rain.

I looked up at the night sky and felt the old mix of wonder and comfort that the stars always bring

me. There was the North Star, cold and bright, and the Dipper, as familiar as my face in a mirror. While riding night herd for the M Cross as a boy, I had learned to time my shift by watching the Dipper as it rolled around the North Star—one complete turn every twenty-four hours.

I thought about Billie, her strength and her decency. Billie was committed to keeping her ranch and her honor, no matter what. She was a lady who inspired loyalty in people, an honest, hard-working woman who cared about her friends and the people who rode for her brand.

I thought about Clem, her father's friend, who loved her. And Maggie, her mother's friend, who bore the weight of a terrible secret in order to spare her.

I thought about Kip Merriday, young, brash, and full of himself—feeding his vain desire to become a gunfighter like Maddox. Not too long ago, I had *been* a kid like Kip. I had run with George Starkweather and his outlaw band until the grace of God set me on a different track. Of all the members of George's gang that I had known, not a single one remained alive. I felt a great sadness, thinking about Kip, but how do you save someone who doesn't want to be saved?

And I thought about Ross Devlin, whose lust for money and power had brought him—and all of us—to that dark hour at the C Heart. How did a man like Ross get to *be* a man like Ross? Was

he *born* with a bent toward evil, or had he earned his ride to hell one step at a time?

It seemed to me then, and it seems to me now, that a man is the result of his choices. He can choose the light and rise to honor and glory, or he can choose darkness and sink into corruption. And sometimes, a man can simply lose his way.

I lost my way after the shooting of Toby Slocum. I turned my back on law enforcement, and set out to find another way of life. I did not expect to live happily ever after like the storybooks say, but I figured I might at least find a calling that did not require the practice of deadly force. Evidently, I figured wrong.

So there I was, hunkered down in a cedar patch beneath the stars with a six-gun on my hip and a rifle in my hands, waiting to kill or be killed. The situation would have been funny if it wasn't so durned serious.

Dawn came slowly, with a faint glow in the east that took its own sweet time in growing brighter. Warm light touched the high spots before the sun appeared, and trees atop the ridges stood out in sharp detail. I was chilled from my night's watch and stiff from sitting on the ground. My feet were numb. Stamping, I tried to bring the feeling back.

At the main house, lamplight glowed in a kitchen window. Wood smoke wafted up into the quiet morning from the stovepipe. Maggie was

already at work in her kitchen, and I knew the coffee would be on. I drew the Winchester's hammer back to half cock, cradled it in the crook of my arm, and started down toward the house.

That's when I saw it. A quick flash of reflected light. Movement atop the eastern hills! Realizing I was skylined on the ridge, I dropped to a squat and raised the binoculars to my eyes. And then I saw—*riders!* A dozen at least, coming fast down the slope toward the ranch's east gate!

Below, at the house, others also saw the riders. Billie was outside, a rifle in one hand as she set the ranch triangle clanging with the other.

Beside the gateway, some two hundred yards away, lay a mounded dirt pile that hid a bundle of capped dynamite. I raised the Winchester and drew a careful bead. Taking a deep breath, I let the air out slowly. I squeezed the trigger and the rifle butt smacked my shoulder. My bullet struck a foot to the right as the lead riders poured in through the gate. Quickly, I levered in a second cartridge and fired again.

The exploding dynamite rang loud in my ears, even six hundred feet away. Dirt and rock blew upward in a geyser of smoke and dust, and I saw two riders and their horses go down. Riders to their rear raced past them, dividing into separate groups beyond the barn lot. I watched four of them splash through the creek and ride hard across the hay meadows.

Clem was firing from the barn loft, and some of the riders were shooting back. I watched one man light a torch and hurl it inside the barn. Ross Devlin, Maddox, and Kip Merriday had been among the first men through the gate, and they located me on the hillside. Ross reined his horse sharply to the right, dismounting on the fly. His face was ashen and his eyes were open wide. Kip was shooting rapidly with a six-gun, but his shots were wild. Maddox drew rein and fired at me with his revolver. A bullet tore into the sod beside me; I felt a second bullet graze my cheek.

A rifle shot rang out from somewhere near the house. Turning, I saw Hitch limping into the fray, shooting at Maddox as he came.

The barn was ablaze but Clem was still firing. I saw the puffs of white smoke that marked his location, as well as the regulators who were returning his fire. Clem must have struck the dynamite bundle we buried at the meadows with a bullet. Again an ear-splitting blast threw sod, smoke, fire and rock toward the sky and men and horses fell.

A bullet struck Maddox's horse! The animal screamed, a high-pitched squeal of shock and pain, and fell kicking on its side in the dirt. Trapped in the open, Maddox spun and dropped Hitch with a single shot.

I levered my rifle and fired at Maddox, but he was moving fast and the bullet struck where he

used to be. Kip Merriday was riding to the rescue; I saw him spur his pinto toward Maddox and extend his arm to sweep the gunman up behind him.

But Maddox had other ideas. He took hold of the offered arm and jerked Kip out of the saddle. Swiftly mounting the pinto, Maddox bent low over the animal's neck and rode hell bent for the hills.

Now Kip was trapped in the open. Fifty feet away, he brought his pistol to bear on me, but my leveled Winchester made him see the error of his ways. Kip dropped the weapon and raised his hands. Clem ambled toward us from the barn, and I committed Kip to his care. "Keep an eye on this would-be bad man," I said. "I'm goin' after Maddox."

Rutherford was tied behind the bunkhouse where I left him. The buckskin lifted his head and whinnied when he saw me, and I quickly tightened his cinch and swung into the saddle. Taking a look around as I rode out I saw no sign of Ross Devlin. The barn by then was fully ablaze, flame licking through the roof and black smoke billowing into the clear morning sky. Over toward the bridge, Maggie bent over Hitch. I had no idea how bad he was hit but he was moving, and I hoped for the best.

Maddox was easy to track. I picked up his horse's hoofprints on the other side of the bridge

and followed them as they led away from the ranch and into the open country beyond. At the crest of the first hill, I scanned the land but saw no sign of the gunman or his horse.

I corrected myself. Maddox was not riding *his* horse, he was riding Kip Merriday's horse, and that, I thought, could make all the difference. Kip's taste in horse flesh tended to the showy but soft, and Maddox was forty pounds heavier than Kip. The gunman might hide, but he would not outrun me.

The land ahead was broken and rough, sagebrush-covered hills scarred by deep ravines and brushy draws. Maddox could be hiding in any one of them. I tried to slow Rutherford, but the buckskin fought the bit's control. His blood was up; he had carried me often enough in pursuit of cattle and game, and he knew I was on the hunt. I gave him his head and let him go. "All right, big son," I said. "Go find 'em."

And find 'em he did. Minutes later, Rutherford raised his head and whinnied. Forty yards away, Maddox broke out of a dry wash, whipping and spurring Kip's lathered paint. Turning in the saddle, the big man fired his pistol at me and I felt the wind of the bullet's passing. Then the lathered pinto lost its footing and fell headlong into a hidden washout. Maddox flew free and landed hard in the loose dirt.

Stepping off Rutherford on the run, I was on the

gunman in seconds. He had lost his six-gun in the fall. The weapon lay in the dirt, inches from his groping hand when I cocked my pistol and pointed it at him. "Leave it," I said.

Maddox's cold grey eyes stared, first at me and then back at the fallen gun. He lay sprawled on his side, his right hand near the gun and his left crooked behind his body. The big man bared his teeth in a smile, but hate was plain on his pock-marked face.

"You fooled me," he said. "I took you for a dumb cowpoke. Appears you're a little *more* than that."

His hand relaxed, pulled back. "You hold the high cards," he said. "I'm all through."

He rolled sharply to the right, his left hand flashing from behind his back. I saw the hideaway gun catch daylight and triggered my forty-four. My bullet caught Maddox dead center and put him down forever.

White smoke, acrid and bitter, drifted in the stillness. "Yeah," I said. "You sure are."

Twenty-Five
A RECKONING

When I approached Kip Merriday's horse, the animal was nervous as a cat, and I believe with good reason. The pinto had been rode hard all the way from the Rafter D. It had gone through a gauntlet of gunfire, blazing barns, and dynamite explosions before getting commandeered by a cruel horseman for a wild ride through rough country and a hard fall in a dry wash. Such treatment would have made even the calmest horse twitchy.

And the pony's ordeal wasn't over. After I talked to him awhile and stroked his neck some, I blindfolded the animal with my bandanna and hoisted Maddox's corpse up and across the saddle. Then I stepped up onto Rutherford, took the pinto's reins, and headed back to the ranch.

The barn was still burning when I rode in. Clem was stacking saddles and tack in a big pile away from the fire, and he had Kip Merriday working for him. Clem looked at the pinto's mortal burden and squinted up at me. "Been huntin', I see," he said.

"Didn't you hear? Regulator season opened this mornin'."

Clem lifted Maddox's head by its long white hair and studied the bullet hole in the dead man's forehead. "One shot kill?"

"I got lucky."

Clem rubbed his nose with his forefinger. "I see you didn't field dress him."

"Didn't want to ruin the hide. What are *you* up to?"

"Had to get the saddles and such away from the fire. One of our guests got careless with matches."

I stepped down from Rutherford. "Appears *you* did a little huntin' yourself," I said. "Any luck?"

"Some," Clem replied. "I got two. Dynamite got one."

"And the others?"

"Rode out of here like their shirt tails were on fire. I expect some of 'em are already back home in Texas."

"What about Ross?"

Clem shrugged. "Saw him early in the fight, but not since. Might be he left with the others."

"Might be," I allowed, but it didn't feel right.

Kip Merriday carried an armload of harness out of the flames and added it to the pile.

"I got the man who stole your horse," I said. "Understand he was a friend of yours."

Kip glanced at Maddox's corpse, and then looked quickly down at the ground. "I don't guess he was my friend," he said.

"No," I said. "I don't guess he was."

I looked around. The heat from the burning barn was intense, keeping both man and beast at bay. A beam fell with a crash, sending up a shower of sparks amid rolling clouds of smoke and steam.

Sweat-stained and grimy, Clem concentrated on the work at hand, sorting saddles, harness, horse collars, and hames. A wave of fondness for the old man passed over me. Clem had been bold as a lion, working to ready our defense and risking his life in the fight against the raiders.

Kip brought out a packsaddle and a set of panniers, and disappeared back into the smoke. Clem folded a saddle blanket and placed it on a pile with others.

"How did you get Kip to help you?" I asked.

"Told him I'd kill him if he didn't."

I turned away from the fire, taking inventory. Dead men lay where they'd fallen. Four horses were dead, one near the east gate, two at the hay meadows, and Maddox's horse in the road this side of the bridge.

"How about Hitch?" I asked. "I saw him take a bullet from Maddox."

"Hitch got lucky for a change. Bullet struck the stock of his rifle and put him down. Knocked the wind out of him, but that's all. He's over at the house with Maggie and Billie."

"I'll go check on him," I said. I turned away, and then stopped.

"Clem," I said. "You did a hell of a job today."

Clem looked up from his labors, and for a moment I caught a glimpse of the man beneath his hard-boiled mask. Then he looked quickly away and went back to his sorting.

"I just got mad," he said.

I don't know whether it was from lack of sleep or the let-down after the morning's fight, but as I walked up to the house, I suddenly felt dog-tired and melancholy in my mind. You would think I'd have been in a mood to celebrate, but I wasn't. We had prevailed over the raiders, and we had suffered no losses to speak of. So I can't explain the heaviness of my spirit.

I opened the screen door and stepped inside. I stopped in the entryway, listening. The house was silent as a tomb. "Billie?" I said. "Maggie? Anybody home?"

No answer.

I started up the stairway that led to the kitchen landing. A tread creaked under my weight, sounding loud in the stillness. Of a sudden my mouth was dry. The pulsing of my heart was loud in my ears. Carefully, I slipped my six-gun from its leather and took another step. At the top of the landing, I hesitated. Then I took a deep breath, stepped quickly into the kitchen, and stopped in my tracks.

Billie stared at me from the doorway of her bedroom, her eyes wide and staring. Ross Devlin stood behind her, his left arm tight about her

throat and the pistol in his right hand cocked and pointed at her head. Maggie stood on my left, facing them from her place beside the stove. She reached out her hands as if to help Billie, but was unable to do so. And Hitch Holbrook lay sprawled on the kitchen floor to my right in a spreading pool of his blood.

"Drop it, Fanshaw!" Devlin said. "I'll kill her if you try anything!"

Hitch was alive, but not by much. His eyes were closed, and his breathing seemed ragged and faint. I turned my eyes back to Devlin and placed my six-gun on the floor.

"I believe you," I said. "If you'd shoot a wounded man I don't expect you'd hesitate to murder a woman."

"I was waiting when they came back inside," Devlin said. "Your friend tried to be a hero."

"Hitch didn't have to *try*. He *is* a hero. What are *you?*"

Devlin's handsome face twisted with rage. "*Damn* you, Fanshaw! All my careful plans—come to nothing because of *you!*"

"Which careful plans are we talkin' about here, Devlin? Rustlin' forty pairs of Billie's cattle to put her in a bind? Goin' in cahoots with that money-grubbin' banker to steal her land? Or maybe lynchin' poor old Irv Baker just to throw a scare into his neighbors?"

"Who are you to judge *me,* saddle tramp? *You*

gunned down an innocent boy in Miles City just because you had the power! Well, *I* have the power now—*I'm* giving the orders!"

Keep pushing him, I thought. *Make him take that gun from Billie's head.*

I clenched my fists and took a step toward him. "You're all through, Ross," I said. "Only way you leave here alive is if you kill me!"

I watched his face, seeing my words work on him like a drug. His eyes took on a haunted, desperate look. His nostrils flared. In his neck, a vein throbbed dangerously. The hand that held the cocked revolver trembled.

Ross pushed Billie sharply away, bringing his gun to bear on me! From the corner of my eye I saw Billie fall! Dropping to one knee, I reached for my own gun!

The blast rocked the room, rattling dishes in the cupboard, bouncing back from the walls and ceiling, the sound deeper and flatter than the pistol shot I expected. Throwing myself to one side, I came up with my gun cocked . . .

And saw Maggie holding the shotgun in her work-worn hands, smoke drifting from its twin barrels and thick in the room. Ross slumped against the wall as if pasted there; his head and shoulders riddled by a double charge of buckshot. Blood-spattered plaster fell from the wall, and Ross's six-gun dropped from his lifeless fingers. For a long moment he seemed to hang there like

some gruesome specter, and then he toppled to the floor and lay still.

I turned to Maggie. Putting my arm around her shoulders, I gently took the shotgun from her hands. "It's all right, Mag," I said. "Everything's all right now."

Maggie's sun-browned face was serene as an angel's. Smiling, she raised her head and I knew she was remembering her friend. "For *you,* Becky," she said.

I knelt at Hitch's side. Blood flowed freely down his face. He lay in his bandages, his left arm still suspended in its sling. His eyes were tightly closed, and his lips were locked in a twist that bared his teeth and declared his pain. I've been known to ask stupid questions at times, and I did so then.

"How're you doin', Hitch?"

"How the hell . . . you *think* I'm doin'? Shot . . . three damn times . . . this *week!* Head hurts . . . like a som'bitch. How're *you* doin'?"

"Better than *you.*"

Gently, I parted his hair. Devlin's bullet had cut a clean furrow across his scalp, but had not penetrated his skull. "Just a crease, pardner," I said. "Good thing you're hard-headed."

Hitch grunted. "Take . . . your word for it," he said.

Across from me, Maggie was already kneeling

at Hitch's side. She placed a basin of warm water on the floor beside him, and began to bathe his wounded head.

I stood up and leaned against a counter top. Relief and gratitude flowed through me like a river. The raid was over; the danger had passed. We had prevailed.

Twenty-Six
RETURN TO MILES CITY

We made our way to Miles City that week. Clem drove Jack and Jill as the team drew the wagon up Main Street to the courthouse. Clad in the house dress and sheepskin coat she favored, Maggie sat beside Clem on the wagon seat. Hitch Holbrook huddled in a blanket behind them, his hat perched atop his bandaged head. And on the floor of the wagon bed, the canvas-wrapped bodies of Ross Devlin, Maddox, and two gunmen killed during the raid swayed and shifted with each jolt of the wagon.

Kip Merriday followed on his skittish pinto, his eyes downcast and his expression morose. Flanking the wagon, Billie rode grace, her claybank mare, while I rode Rutherford and led Roanie.

Tom Irvine met us on the courthouse steps. I swung over and dismounted. "Tom," I said. "You're lookin' good, for an old man."

Beneath his graying mustache, Tom's teeth were strong and white. "You, too, Merlin," he said. "But you know what they say. It ain't the years, it's the *mileage*."

Billie drew rein beside me and Tom's smile

widened. "This is Billie Hart," I said. "She owns the C Heart, over on the Mizpah."

Tom took off his hat and smiled. "Ma'am," he said.

"Just 'Billie' will do, Sheriff," she said. "I've heard a great deal about you."

Tom held his smile. "Well, if you heard it from Merlin, I have to warn you. He has a bad habit of telling the truth."

Behind Tom, a lanky deputy with ears that stuck out like the handles on a sugar bowl looked Kip over with a jaundiced eye. I nodded at Kip. "And this is Kip Merriday, the kid I told you about on the telephone. He came along of his own volition. Wants to give himself up."

Tom nodded at the deputy, who took Kip by the arm and led him away. Tom stepped down to street level and looked at Hitch. I made the introductions.

"This feller wearin' the hindoo turban under his hat is Hitch Holbrook. Hitch was a line rider for the Claymore Cattle Company until he joined our merry crew. He could use a doctor, if you can locate one. He's had a hard week. Hitch, meet Tom Irvine, sheriff of Custer County."

The two men shook hands. "There ain't no real hurry about the sawbones, Sheriff," Hitch said. "If the wagon ride here didn't kill me, I expect I'll live forever."

Tom looked into the wagon bed. "And I

suppose these two gents would be Ross Devlin and a gunhawk called Maddox," he said.

"And two of their men," I agreed.

Tom smiled. "I also suppose you'll tell me how they came to be in this condition."

"The truth, the whole truth, as much as you need."

Tom turned away from the wagon. "Can't ask for more than that," he said. Turning to Clem, he said, "Why don't you take the ladies over to the MacQueen house? I'll send Doc Booker down to have a look at you, Hitch. When you boys get the ladies settled, come on back. We'll give these dead fellers a ride to the undertaker."

"Fair enough," said Clem. "Do you suppose a man could find a whiskey someplace?"

With a perfectly straight face, Tom replied, "Why, yes. I believe there's a chance we can find a drink of whiskey *someplace* in Miles City."

I smiled. Seeing as there were more than four dozen saloons in Miles City at the time, there seemed to be a *good* chance.

As it turned out, Tom and me didn't even have to *go* to a saloon for a drink. While we awaited Clem's return, Tom took a quart of Confederate Dew from a desk drawer and poured us each a splash in the office coffee mugs. "You've heard of a tempest in a teapot?" Tom asked. "Well, this here is a tornado in a coffee mug. Here's how!"

We sat together at Tom's desk. "Before the

waters get muddied by lawyers, preachers, and what-not," he said, "I'd like to hear the whole story from you."

"All right," I said. "Do you want my sworn deposition?"

"Hell no. Just tell me."

And tell him I did, from the day I left my badge behind and rode off into the Big Open to the present moment. "That's pretty much all of it, Tom. Two of the hired guns were killed in the fight at the C Heart—three, counting Maddox—and maybe two in the raid on Hitch Holbrook."

Tom looked at me over the rim of his mug. "Devlin shot Holbrook?"

I nodded. "Devlin led the raid on the C Heart. He panicked when he found us ready for him, and ready to put up a fight. Devlin hid out in Billie's house until she went back inside. When she did, he took her as a hostage. Hitch tried to protect her and got grazed by a bullet for his trouble."

"Nobody's going to give a damn about the *pistoleros*," Tom said, "but there may be a few questions asked about Devlin's death. Tell me again—how did he die?"

"Ross Devlin held a gun to Billie Hart's head in the kitchen of her house. Billie shook him loose and a shotgun took him out—both barrels of a twelve gauge."

Tom placed his coffee mug on his desk and smoothed his mustache with a thumb and

forefinger. He laced his fingers across his belly and leaned back in his swivel chair. "You say Devlin threw down on you when Billie broke free. So you killed him in self defense, right?"

I hesitated. "What if it didn't happen *exactly* that way? How much do you *really* want to know?"

Tom leaned forward again and placed his elbows on the desk. "Well," he said. "I was just wondering. You said Devlin got the drop on you and made you lay your gun down. Then Billie broke free somehow and Devlin got his head blown off by a shotgun. Where did you get the shotgun?"

Again, I thought before I answered. "Just suppose for the sake of argument that Devlin was *not* killed in a shoot-out with me. Suppose someone *else* killed him to protect a *third* party."

It was Tom's turn to take an extra moment to think. I watched as he ran the pictures of the showdown at Billie's house through his mind. "You mean 'someone' like one of the women?"

"Just supposin'," I said.

Tom sat up straight in his chair and poured a second splash of whiskey in our mugs. "In that case," he said, "I hereby declare that Merlin Fanshaw killed the aforesaid Ross Devlin in self defense during an attack at Billie Hart's ranch. Fanshaw acted in his official capacity as U.S. deputy marshal and is to be commended for

his resourcefulness and courage. Amen and hallelujah."

"Thanks, Tom," I said. "You once told me that makin' trouble for a good man for *doin'* good wasn't in the public interest. I'd say that would apply to a good *woman,* too."

Tom raised his mug in salute. "So would I," he said.

Tom sat down sidesaddle on his desk top. "As it happens," he said, "Yours ain't the only complaint against Ross Devlin I've heard lately. His former cow boss, Sam Bodie, passed through Miles City a week ago and paid me a visit."

I never had liked whiskey much, but Tom's Confederate Dew was beginning to grow on me. I took a sip and felt it warm me from scalp to heels.

I nodded. "Bodie and me had our ups and downs. He stopped by to see me the day he quit the Rafter D."

"Ups and downs, you say. Such as?"

"A while back Devlin had Kip Merriday tie down a Rafter D steer to make it look like a rustler was workin' the range. I happened on the scene just after Kip lit out, and Sam Bodie and Devlin's men happened on *me.*

"Bodie figured he'd caught himself a real live cow thief. He knocked me down, put a rope on me, and hung me from a tree. I'd have crossed the great divide sure if Hitch Holbrook hadn't

showed up. Hitch threw down on the necktie party and told Bodie to turn me loose. Said he'd seen the real rustler, a feller in a black hat and checkered shirt, ride out just before I showed up.

"He'd seen Kip Merriday, of course, but nobody knew it was Kip at the time. Anyway, Bodie strung me up and I took it personal.

"When I'd healed up some, I ran across Bodie at the barbershop in Fairfax. I lodged an objection to the way he'd done me. I lodged it with both my hands and feet, and I throwed his six-gun in a water trough.

"Bodie quit Devlin a week later. Came by the C Heart to see me and mend some fences. He said Devlin was out to run all the small operators off the range and take over Billie's spread, no matter *what* he had to do. Then, just before he left, he told me the regulators aimed to kill a friend of mine. I asked who that might be, and he said it was Hitch Holbrook.

"The fight was already underway when I got to Hitch's camp. I opened up on Devlin's men from a ridgetop and they lit out for a more peaceful climate. I took Hitch back to the C Heart, where Maggie and Billie doctored him. But I already told you that."

"You did," said Tom, "but it was good to hear you tell it the same way twice. Most witnesses tell me a different story every time I ask."

Tom turned back from the window. "What do

you figure you'll do now, Merlin? You aim to stay with the C Heart?"

I thought about Tom's question. Hesitant and halting, I let my thoughts drift to that long ago night with Tom at the bank and was surprised to find that Toby Slocum's ghost no longer haunted me. I would never forget and always regret Toby's death at my hand, but his unquiet spirit seemed to be at rest at last.

In that dark place in my mind where guilt and remorse once dwelt, an older memory lived. I recalled Chance Ridgeway's face and heard his voice as he shared his own reason for living.

"I have made it my life's work to keep the snakes from doin' harm to the robins," he said. "I still see things in terms of good and evil, right and wrong, and while I may sometimes bend the law, I never cut evil any slack."

Tom was waiting, his expression serious and his gaze intense. He had asked me a question I couldn't answer at the time. Now I could.

"I thought I might see if Ridgeway will give me my deputy's badge back," I said.

Billie, Maggie, Hitch, Clem, and me met at the MacQueen House that night for supper in the hotel's dining room. Billie and Maggie wore stylish dresses of brocaded silk, complete with ruffles, ribbons, and bustles, and they had put their hair up in what they said was the latest style. You'd have thought they were visiting ladies

from Chicago or New York City, and they sure looked beautiful by lamplight.

Clem had spent some time that day in the barber's chair and his skin glowed pink as a wild rose. The unnatural brightness of his eyes and the rosy glow of his nose told me he'd also spent some time at a local saloon. I had bought a new shirt and a stiff collar to mark the occasion. We were chipper as larks and playful as otters.

By mutual agreement, no one spoke of the violent times just past or mentioned that we would soon be parting. Come morning I would board a train for Helena and a meeting with Chance Ridgeway. Billie would return to the C Heart to rebuild her herd and her life. Maggie would again rule the kitchen in her house dress and sheepskin coat, smoking cigarettes, and cooking for ranch hands. Clem would look after the ladies, fussing and fuming at bankers, the weather, and all misfortune, and in the evenings drink a little whiskey.

We dined that night on pheasant, or what passed for pheasant. We laughed and teased and made jokes out of the deep well of our mutual affection. We raised our glasses and drank champagne. When at last our supper ended and Billie stood on tiptoe to kiss me good-night and good-bye, I felt a glow that would last through all the days ahead, knowing I had family on Mizpah Creek in the Big Open.

Center Point Large Print
600 Brooks Road / PO Box 1
Thorndike ME 04986-0001 USA

(207) 568-3717

US & Canada:
1 800 929-9108
www.centerpointlargeprint.com